MW00618404

ALL THE BEST!

1

The

Bakken

by

L. J. Martin

Wolfpack Publishing
48 Rock Creek Road
Clinton, Montana 59825

ISBN: 978-1-62918-124-0

Print Edition
Copyright 2014 L. J. Martin

Wolfpack Publishing
48 Rock Creek Road
Clinton, Montana 59825

ISBN: 978-1-62918-124-0

Chapter One

Three of them are standing outside, in the dark, smoking. But it's hard to tell if it's smoke they're exhaling, or just hot breath into frigid air...icicles are already a foot long on the eaves of the building.

Smokers get a little grumpy having to go outside into mustache-freezing air to corrode their lungs and these three don't look happy. Two of them look like Indians; the third one who's eyeballing me like I'm something stuck to his shoe is a dirty blond white-eye with stringy hair to his shoulders and is the largest of the three at an easy two sixty—he's got at least forty pounds on me, although we're about equal height. And he's the ugliest of the trio, and that's saying something—dog-butt-ugly comes to mind.

As I near them, I can smell the dirty coveralls, the scarred steel toed boots covered with scum, and the oil spotted Carhartt jackets they all wear; and an even stronger odor, the cheap weed they're smoking and passing around.

"What the fuck are you looking at?" the big ol' boy—who's gripping a half inch long hooter with the fingernails of his index finger and thumb—asks as I brush past and head for the front door. I can see this is going to be a fun place to work, if you enjoy the occasional busted knuckle...or worse.

"Not very fucking much," I say over my shoulder, and push through the door without giving him a chance to figure out it was a slam.

I hear him yell after me, "Eat me, asshole."

I've been in town fifteen minutes, and am glad I took my new employer's advice—and fat advance—and bought a truck and camper before heading out to America's fasting growing boomtown...Williston, North Dakota. Why would a berg in this God-forsaken place—it's December 12th and ten degrees outside—be growing so fast? Oil...to be more specific, shale oil, is the reason, and oil is money, and jobs, and much of the U.S. is still on its ass. And those who truly want to work will go damn near anywhere to do so, particularly for big money.

Jobs and money! Why else would a place so friggin' cold have grown from twelve thousand five hundred population to thirty five thousand in thirteen years?

A dozen years ago Williston was a small town with half the population hard working folks of Norwegian descent, mostly in farming or related jobs. Man, has it ever changed.

Why the camper? Because even the old folks home has been converted to rooms for rent by the week, six hundred a week—the old folks were sent packing. Get in your wheelchair and hit the road, gramps, it's boomtown time. Camp spots are almost as expensive, but I'm parking my new abode for free, thanks to Owens-McKittrick Oil Well Service Company, with whom I've accepted a contract to do a little search and destroy work. That's a trade for which I've been well trained, thanks to the United States Government and the Marine Corps.

Like all my 'contracts' this one is verbal, as my kind of work is not the kind folks like having leave paper trails.

I've been driving for fifteen hours starting this morning with the sun not yet over the Wasatch Range, from Salt Lake City where I spent the night after driving from Las Vegas, where I occasionally hang my hat.

Having spent most of the last eight years in cheap motel rooms or worse, I'm beginning to like my new camper, a place where I know where a few things are stowed. Some of the rest of my belongings, which are spread out in mini-storage facilities in Ventura, Las Vegas, and Sheridan, Wyoming, have been consolidated into a ten foot enclosed Wells Cargo trailer which tows nicely behind my camper and new F250 diesel. A good portion of the trailer is taken up with a Harley Sportster, which may be a little crazy as icy North Dakota roads don't lend themselves to two-wheel transportation.

It's nine p.m., colder than the proverbial well digger's ass—and that's a metaphor that works well in Williston—and scheduled to get a lot colder tonight if you can believe WDAY TV, and I'm hungry and need some fuel for my personal internal fire. I haven't eaten since I grabbed a dog in a mini-mart where I fueled up in Billings, Montana, where I also took an hour to wander Cabelas and pick up some cold weather gear. I passed this roadhouse on the way in, Big Rosie's, which sports a simulated oilfield pumping unit with her neon sign going up and down, along with a skimpy dressed mannequin—bikini and cowboy hat—riding it like it was a bucking bull machine. How could the food not be good in a classy joint like that?

In the morning I'm due to meet with my former CO from Desert Storm days, who's now my employer, but I might as well get to work as I've been hired to freelance and get rid of the drug trade—my employer thinks the locals are in a little over their heads, which has been well demonstrated by the continued problem. Drug use is costing Owens-McKittrick a lot of money in injuries—Workman's Comp for the oil well service trade is already among the highest of any trade—lost work time, busted up equipment, and liability, and where better to begin work than in a roadhouse that looks like you'd have to be high on something to frequent the joint. Besides when I passed the establishment on the way in there was room to park in the lot, which has to be an expansive two acres, and not many places in Williston seem to be able to make that claim, at least after my quick trip though town to check it out.

The joint is jam-packed, ten men or more to each lady, and that includes the girls working the tables. Willy is blaring out *Good Hearted Woman* loud enough that most have to shout to be heard by those at their same table. And most the men look like they wish they were back home in Kansas with their good hearted woman.

Like the three outside, the place reeks of petroleum as it's hard to work in the patch without getting occasionally doused in either crude, or fuel oil, or grease from the plethora of equipment. A truck stop I passed out on Highway 2 on the way in told the tale: mud pumping trucks, oil well service tool trucks, trailers loaded with drill pipe, cranes, and on and on. Out of five dozen rigs only one was a hay truck.

There's not a vacant table in the place, but there is a place to stand at the bar, so I do, and luckily the guy to my right gets up and leaves and I grab his stool and order a bottle of Trout Slayer, a decent beer, and look for a menu.

The bartender is a rough edged old girl with thinning red hair, probably died, who looks to be past her prime as a hooker, although this crowd would probably pay handsomely even for her should she want to return to the trade. She eyes me up and down, my leather coat is way too light for this weather, and she notices.

"If you hung your real coat by the door, keep an eye on it. Things get wings 'round here." She gives me a wink, and I'm a little surprised she can with the amount of eye shadow she has caked over the wrinkles.

"Locked in the truck, thanks. What's good?"

"Besides me," she says, and I get another wink. Maybe she still is a working girl.

"No question in my mind you're the best, but I mean what's to eat."

"Besides me," she says again, and guffaws before she continues, "the Fracker is a winner and if you eat it all you don't have to pay the twenty five bucks it costs."

"Sounds like a hell of a deal, but I'm watching my waistline. How about a club sandwich?"

"You ain't got much waistline compared to those shoulders," she says and gives me another wink, then turns as someone down the bar yells.

"Hey, Maggy, how about another fuckin' beer. Or are you thru for the night?"

"Keep your pants on, peterhead. It's coming."

I have the beer half gone before the guy next to me on my right spins on his stool and asks, "You new to town?"

I nod, eyeballing the pock-face guy and noting the puckered scar from the left side of his nose to the edge of his mouth. I can see that he's had a bad laser job trying to remove a couple of prison tat tears from below his eye.

"Got work yet?" he asks. He's a hatchet faced old boy, with an Elvis Presley doo, ugly as an anteater, but upscale for this place in clean pressed jeans and a decent shirt under a buttoned brown leather vest, and I note a bulge on the left side, it's a concealed carry vest. He's sitting on a sheepskin coat, the kind with wool puffing out the sleeves and around the collar, that's draped over his barstool, and I note a little glimpse of blue steel in one of the coat pockets. This guy is loaded for bear.

"Not yet," I say, only a small lie as I meet with my ex-CO and conclude my deal tomorrow.

"You're big enough to eat hay and shit in the road...I can get you on a couple of places. Have you worked the patch before?"

I guess that's supposed to be a back-handed compliment. I'm heavier than he is, but about equal tall. "I'm gonna hang tight until I check things out." I give him a nod and turn back to my beer, but he continues.

"You looking to get some pussy?"

I smile at him and shrug. "Normally that'd be a big ol' yes...but I just came from Vegas. Got my ashes hauled from there to next month."

"How about a little tweek?"

Didn't take me long to get a line on the dope trade in Williston. My first time covering a bar stool and I get offered a little crystal meth or crack, whichever he considers material for 'a little tweek.'

He eyes me up and down, then adds, "You're not the law, are you?"

"Fuck no," I snap. I do carry a bail enforcement badge, a bounty hunter's brass, but it's locked away in my trailer, along with my arsenal, the tools of my trade. He might be concerned about the .40 cal Glock in the small of my back, or the extendable baton in my inside jacket pocket, but I reply with indignation, "Do I look like the friggin' law to you?"

"Hard to tell these days. You like young pussy?" he asks, since I denied being the law.

Again I snarl, "I ain't the law, and I ain't no fuckin' fag...of course I like young pussy. Do I look like a fucking fag to you?"

He shakes his head knowingly, then says, "You may have had your ashes hauled by that sloppy only-hit-one-edge-at-a-time strap-a-board-on-your-ass-to-keep-from-falling-in gash in Vegas, but I'm talking primo prime fifteen year old pussy fresh from Russia so tight it'll make you cry-for-mercy pussy. You want some of that?"

The barmaid sits my sandwich down, "Another beer, big boy?" she asks.

"Sure," I reply, and, although I can feel the adrenalin creep up my backbone, add, "and buy my buddy here one."

"Oh, yeah," he says, but waits for her to move away before continuing. "How about it. Two hundred will get you fifteen minutes of prime grade A sweet as sage-honey poontang."

I take a bite of the club, chew, and act as if I'm considering his offer. Then swallow and turn to him. "Tempting as hell, but I'd better hang onto my dough until I get hooked up with work."

"I told you, I can get you forty bucks an hour...roustabout work...and have you on a payroll by ten A.M. tomorrow."

I take a swig of beer as the barmaid places another in front me and one in front of my new 'buddy.' Then as she moves away, I ask, "Is there anything you can't do?"

"Not fucking much," he says with a crooked grin.

I stick out my hand. "I'm John Meoff...friends call me Jack."

He rears back a little. "You're fuckin' with me...."

I laugh. "Yeah, I am. It's Dick...Dick Strong," I lie again, as it's actually Mike Reardon. This time he shakes hands. "You got a name?" I ask, since he doesn't offer.

"Yeah, but you don't need it." And I bought the asshole a six buck beer.

"I hear a little Texas twang in there?"

He gets a little defensive. "George Bush has one too. Could be Louisiana or Alabama. Don't mean shit."

I shrug, and go back to my sandwich as he turns to the guy on his right. He's obviously tight with the guy, who's as big as a hog's head barrel, looks twice as dumb, and is as bald as the proverbial bowling ball...but hatchet nose is leaning right in, talking low to the dude. It's obvious they're tight, and don't want to be overheard.

I dig my iPhone out and act like I'm checking my email, but turn the camera feature on and reverse it so it takes a pic from the front rather than the back, turn my back to him a little and over my shoulder, get a flashless pic of him as he takes a swig of his beer, then I reverse the function, turn back facing the bar, and get a pic of him in the mirror behind the bar, a profile as he talks to the guy on his right, then one of the big bald boy.

I finish my second beer and my sandwich, pay with cash, leave a generous tip, and get up to go. Hatchet face turns back and suggests, "When you get that first fat paycheck and have a pocket full of hundreds, come on back. I'm usually here by ten or eleven, and if you hurry, that young twat won't be stretched out yet."

I notice his teeth appear good, so it's a sure thing he's only selling, not using.

"Can't wait," say. It's all I can do not to put a chop from the back-hard-edge of my hand into his protruding Adams apple, but it wouldn't do to be taken up on manslaughter charges before I solved my old CO's problems…and I probably wouldn't quit until this asshole bought the farm, if the first cut didn't smash his larynx and kill him. Nothing I hate more than child molesters, and this fuck-face is one if he's peddling fifteen year olds. I'll keep him in mind. In fact near the top of the list.

As I start away the old redhead yells after me, "Thanks, big boy. Y'all come on back and see me."

I wave over my shoulder. Elbowing my way through the crowd, I shove out the front door, and only walk about twenty feet before I realize two of the three guys who were standing by the door when I came in are now three rows of cars away, and standing at the rear of my trailer.

It's been a long day, but I guess it's not over.

I slip between a black Dodge van and a white crew-cab F250 pick up truck, and lean back against the van and watch. And sure as hell, the third guy, the biggest-ugliest one, saunters up with a pair of two foot long bolt cutters in one hand and a tire iron in the other. I smile as the trailer is not only locked with a hardened built-in door lock, but has a hardened chain and padlock securing it as well.

I have on crepe soled high top shoes and can move quietly for a big guy—a survival tactic well learned as Marine Recon moving around the streets of Iraq where a crunch of gravel might attract a spray from an AK 47—and do so approaching the three of them as the big one tries the bolt cutters on the chain and one of the Indians tries prying the door with the tire iron.

The one who's only watching is standing up straight, his back to me, so the extendable baton catches him at the base of the skull on vertebrae one, and he goes down like the sack of shit he is. The big boy looks up from his work on the chain in surprise, his eyes wide as I crack him across the bridge of the nose—the crunch of bone is palpable. He drops the bolt cutters and reels back, grasping his nose with both hands as it's doing a great imitation of a fire hose, spouting blood through his fingers.

The other one, the one with the tire iron, manages to back away enough to be facing me, and ready for my attack. He raises the tire iron, and to his credit, charges forward, but his out cold buddy is in his way, and he stumbles over him enough that he goes down on one hand. He's wearing a knit cap, but it's not nearly enough as I bring the baton down dead center on his pate. He's still coming forward, but his eyes have rolled up in his head and I step aside and he makes three steps past me before he goes to his knees, the tire iron dropped. Just for the hell of it, as I know he's finished unless he has cast-iron for a skull, I kick him between the shoulder blades and he goes to his face, unmoving.

I spin back, although I don't think the big boy will want much more, and take a step his way. He does the scalded-ass-ape and gravel is flying behind his heels as he heads for Canada, or wherever.

Doing a quick scan around, I see that two more guys have come out of the joint and are only a row away, but they're merely watching, arms folded, enjoying the spectacle.

One of them steps forward and I see it's the child molester, old hatchet face; and he's with the beer-barrel-big bald boy who was next to him at the bar. A bodyguard, I'd guess from the way he keeps scanning his surroundings; either that or he's watching nervously for the cops.

"You sure you're not a cop?" hatchet face calls out.

"Sure I'm a cop. My whole department is in this trailer, along with three squad cars."

He laughs. Then asks, "Hey, I'll give you a job. You ever bodyguard?"

"No thanks," I say, and fold the baton and head for the door to my truck.

"If you change your mind, I'm here fuckin' near every night."

I wave over my shoulder. *Yeah, you are, asshole, and I'll make sure I find you before I finish this job and leave town.*

Chapter Two

Lt. Col. Oscar Fuerenstein still looks like an active duty Marine, with close cropped hair, formerly blond now gone gray, a neck that flares from his ears to his shoulders like an upside down martini glass, and a penchant to down ten of them, with more than a dash of Vermouth, at a setting. I've seen him add an injured Marine's seventy pound pack to his own seventy pound pack, and finish a twenty mile hump back to base.

A hell of a man.

And he's grinning from ear to ear as he strides out of his office, across the reception area of the double wide trailer—one of a half-dozen in the complex—that serve as the offices of Owens-McKittrick Oil Well Service Company.

He extends a hand that looks like it might have been carved from stone, and shakes mine with a grip like coiled steel.

"How are you, colonel," I ask, and can't help but grin myself. He was one of the few who stood up for me at my court martial, and was probably the reason I received a general rather than the full boat and a few years in Leavenworth. You're not supposed to frag Iraqi civilians much less an Iraqi Major General who was in the wrong place at the wrong time…even if they were all involved in the stoning of a couple of innocent young women.

But I'd do it all over again.

"It's Oscar now, Mike. Come on it and I'll fill you in on the Bakken debacle."

I follow him into a rather sparse office and find a seat across the desk.

"I know, I know," he says as he sits and notes me looking the place over, "it's not Madison Avenue, but trust me, it's throwing off plenty of dough. The Bakken is gonna save this country from having to kiss more *Haji* ass. I hear you've been leading an exciting life, at least that's what Skip reports?" Skip was another jarhead in our unit, and the guy who got me back in touch with my old CO and this job, and who was partnered up with me on my last job.

I shrug, as a girl enters with a pot and two cups.

The Colonel introduces us, "Mike, Amber," and I stand and extend a hand. She's almost as tall as me, must be six feet, of course she has on at least three-inch heels. Her eyes aren't amber, but ice blue, her hair leans to the copper side of blond, and her bountiful bust line is straining at the sweater she wears. She's no spring chicken, about my age…a couple of years one side or the other of forty. But lookin' good! The colonel must do his own hiring.

She shakes with polite indifference, pours, asks, "Cream or sugar?" and I shake my head no, and she exits, and watching her exit is as pleasurable as watching her enter.

So I ask, "You must do the hiring around here?"

He laughs, and shakes his head no. "Just the luck of the draw. I'll tell you, for a little town, the local girls are flat out beautiful. Must be all that good Norwegian stock. However, they're way outnumbered now by the whores and female hustlers. Boomtowns have a way…."

So I get serious. "So, what's worth and a twenty five thou retainer and a hundred grand fee to Owens-McKittrick?"

I can see his jaw tighten before he answers. "Dope, like I said on the phone, is rampant here in North Dakota and in eastern Montana, and it's costing us big time. Accidents, downtime, Workman's Comp, all of it, and I want some of the scumbags who are cooking this meth crap and importing grass and God knows what else to get run out of dodge. How far, is up to you…and the local cops are way over their heads. I just had one of our best tool pushers busted for statutory, even though he was paying for it…and the kid he was dipping got turned over to immigration."

I nod. "Yeah, I got offered a fifteen year old last night, and some dope. My ass hadn't hit the stool for a minute before the guy next to me was working me."

"Rosie's?"

"How'd you guess?"

"It's the worst place in town and just outside the city limits. I think the local PD is okay, but I worry about the sheriff's department."

"On the take?"

He shrugs. "Maybe you can find out. A good part of our operations are in this county, so it's important. We have three crew camps with over two hundred beds each, all in the county."

"So, when do I go to work?"

"The moment you step out that door, but I don't think it's wise if you step back in. Keep as far from Owens-McKittrick as possible. Sorry, but it has to be that way. We don't know you...you don't know us."

"I'm used to it. It's SOP in my line. You said I had a place to park a camper or trailer...I bought a truck and camper, and am towing an equipment trailer."

He laughs. "You need a trailer full of equipment?"

"Colonel, you don't want to know."

"No rockets or mortars, I hope," and he laughs again.

"Home made, if there are," I smile...like I said, it's best he doesn't know.

"We've got a lot next to an equipment yard. A house burned down there two years ago and we put in four RV hookups using the water and septic that used to serve the house. We've got one space there, and it's yours. Tell anyone who asks that you're renting. Amber will give you a map. And here's a little reading for you...." He hands me an inch thick binder.

"How do I keep in touch?"

"I've got a throw away phone just for that reason," he hands me a slip with the number. Then adds, "Mike, we've had three dozen deaths in the patch so far this year, a few of them related to booze or dope, and more than a few of them at the hand of another human. Keep an eye on your six."

I smile and nod as if it goes without saying. "Nice seeing you, Colonel—"

"Oscar."

"Yes, sir, I'll try. You may not hear from me for a week or more."

"Don't get hurt," he says, "some of these assholes play rough. I've had all the KIA's I want."

I laugh quietly. "If they didn't play rough you wouldn't need me. I left the Queensbury Rules back in high school…as you well know."

I give him a sloppy salute that would have had me doing KP ten years ago, and head out to where the tall copper-blond is working at a computer.

She looks up over half-glasses. "So, Mr. Reardon—"

"Mike."

"So, Mike, are you hired?"

I shrug. "Guess not, but I got a place to park my camper if that counts. I guess it pays to have served with the boss…he said you'd give me a map."

Giving her my most devastating smile, I take it from her well-manicured hand and start to leave.

"Hey, Mike, if you like a great steak, DiAngelo's has the best Italian in North Dakota, and great steaks."

"Thanks, I'll give it a try," I say, and turn again.

And again she calls after me, "And good music and a dance floor."

That stops me short. "And do you dance?" I ask.

"Like a dream, you?" Her smile is far more devastating than mine.

"Probably more like a nightmare, but I'm willing…"

"See you around," she says, and gives me a wink.

That calls for another smile in return, and I give her a nod and head out.

The camper has electric jacks so I have it off the truck and dropped and the trailer parked next to it in minutes after driving to the east side of town and finding the place. I lock a ball into the hitch on the trailer to make it more difficult to steal, and sit a caltrop in front and rear of each tire, so if someone manages to get the trailer hooked up, both tires will instantly be blown. The snow hides the razor sharp caltrops nicely. I keep a box full of the devices under my seat just in case I'm pursued and want to put a stop to it.

One of the neighboring RV's is actually an old school bus with passenger windows painted out, obviously owned by a flower child—hard to picture one in the old patch—as it's covered with paintings and peace signs, another is a forty foot trailer with three cars parked next to it, and the third is a Lance camper much like mine. The forlorn foundation of the house is still on the front of the lot, and the rear is taken up by the RV's and a storage shed.

I can see that I'm not quite prepared as the water risers are covered with insulation and have electric heat tape circling them not only above but on into the underground portion. Won't do me any good to hook up without insulation and electric tape on my hose. I note that even the expandable sewer hoses from the other rigs are insulated. This means a trip to the hardware store before I hook up.

Good thing I made note of the Ace Hardware on 26th Street as I did my quick turnaround last night. Fact was, after not finding a place to hook up, I spent the night in their parking lot, until a cop rapped on my door, startling me awake like I was holed up in a bass drum. He woke me at 4 A.M. He was kind enough to direct me to an all-night coffee shop but duty bound enough to run me off, informing me that the whole town would be covered with campers and trailers if they didn't keep a handle on things. It took me twenty minutes to get the ice off my windows so I could drive. Damn if Williston is not making Las Vegas look a little like Shangri-La.

I pick up heat tape, extension cords, a snow shovel, a small electric heater and—taking note of how my neighboring RV's are set up—a dozen bales of straw to rim the bottom of the camper, and spend another hour working my site down to the soil and rimming my temporary home.

It's lunch time before I get settled in enough so the cold doesn't shut down my living arrangements, so I sneak out to see if the recommended DiAngelo's serves lunch…and they do.

The place is a little upscale for my taste, dark wood, red velvet, but if women like the beautiful Amber hang out there I might make an exception. They do make a hell of a sausage sandwich, so I stuff one in, and since I don't plan to come face to face with any bad guys for a while, knock down a half bottle, a split, of Zinfandel.

I've left the little electric heater working in the camper and expect it'll be toasty by the time I get back and since it'll probably be nights I'm working, and I've enjoyed a fat sandwich, some good wine, and a warm camper's waiting…I decide a nap is in order.

Tonight I think I'll head back and cozy up to my new buddy, hatchet face.

Chapter Three

It's six PM by the time I roll out of my cab-over bed and pull on a knit cap that covers the ears, a clean plaid hunting shirt, fleece lined jeans, all over new Under Armour long John's. My leather jacket and then a butt length good-to-twenty-below North Face jacket almost completes the outfit...my .40 cal Glock and the proven-useful extendable baton clipped to my belt does so. Luckily I can remove the North Face and the jacket still serves to hide the Glock. I'm so used to Military style boots that I almost feel naked without them, but I've bought a pair of thousand gram Thinsulate hunting books that are lots warmer. Although my crepe soles are quiet as hell, they're a little out of place in a steel-toe world, and low cuts are way to damn cold.

I have a concealed carry permit, issued by an old friend and schoolmate who's now the Sheriff of Sheridan County and who lives in my hometown of Sheridan, Wyoming, which allows me to carry, technically in thirty six states, but I'm sure as in most concealed carry states it's not legal to have a loaded firearm in a place that serves booze. In fact, the baton is illegal in many states, even on the street, where the firearm is good to go. Only when the odds are very bad do I produce either...then again I don't want to take a knife to a gunfight. Been there, done that, and have an in and out scar in my side to prove it.

It's nice to have the truck free of the camper and trailer, there's a lot more spring in her step, but I'd rather be riding the Harley. I plan to get the tires studded so I have a chance on the ice and will take care of that tomorrow. But I still won't ride unless it's an emergency.

DiAngelo's was such great food I decide to try it again, and as I suspected when I had lunch there, it's an after hours bar as well as a great restaurant. There aren't many neckties in all of Williston, but those that are worn here seem to all be gathered at the long dark wood bar, as are the women who might be attracted to the town's bankers, attorneys, and accountants. In Jeans, plaid shirt, and hunting boots, I don't exactly fit in, but as I sip my beer, a few of the old boys from the oil patch begin to filter in...although even they aren't the oil stained grease spotted bunch that Rosie's attracts. These guys are middle management and above, some dressed not but a step-up from my attire, but clean. The bar was only half full when I entered, but it's filled up and there's not an empty stool, and a line of folks standing behind those sitting.

I'm deep in thought when someone pokes me in the ribs, and I spin on the bar stool to come face to face with a beautiful copper blond.

"Amber."

"The music doesn't start until nine," she says, and gives me one of those brilliant smiles that would melt a weaker man and only make my knees go a little weak.

"Love to try and stay off your toes but I've got something scheduled." The fact is the colonel asked me to stay away from Owens-McKittrick, and I presume that meant from Owens-McKittrick employees as well...damn it.

She laughs. "Didn't take you long to hook up in Williston, and with twenty men to every eligible female."

I can't help but grin. "Thanks for the vote of confidence, but it's not that kind of scheduled entertainment. Can I buy you one drink before I get out of here." She nods, and I ask, "What's your pleasure?"

"That might take a while to explain...but to drink I'll take a Cosmo."

I turn and wave to the bartender. "Cosmo."

"Up or rocks," he asks. I didn't know they came on the rocks, but turn back.

"Up, of course," she says.

I slip off the stool. "Climb up here."

"I didn't come over to bum a drink or to run you off your seat."

"My mama, God rest her soul, would slap me silly if I let a lady stand while I sat on my lazy butt."

She climbs up on the stool, and crosses her legs, showing enough perfectly tanned thigh that I get a jolt to my groin. I sigh deeply, and silently damn Colonel Oscar Fuerenstein.

"There you are, Amber?" the voice comes from over my shoulder and I turn to see a guy about my height, and as wide, dressed like he's modeling in *GQ*. He's eyeballing me like a bull at a bastard calf.

"Great, Tony. How are things at the PD?"

"Busy."

She nods to me, but says to him. "Say hello to Mike."

The guy sticks out a slender but strong hand and we shake.

"Tony DiAngelo," he says.

"Mike Reardon," I offer, not liking to give my real name, but Amber started it. Then I follow up, "DiAngelo,...this your joint?"

"My old man's joint. I'm with the police department."

"Plain clothes...detective?" I ask.

"That's it. How about you, Mike?"

"Kicking around looking for work. Heard this was the place to find it."

"You can get on in the old patch in a blink of the eye if that's what you want. Hell, McDonald's is paying a three hundred buck signing bonus...not that you look like a burger flipper."

His tone is a little smartass and I think it's a subliminal insult, but let it slide, and smile with my reply. "I've done worse."

"Well, good luck," he says, and I don't think very sincerely, then he turns again to Amber. "I'm buying supper if you're ready." Then he turns back to me, "Don't get any ideas...she loves to make me jealous."

She giggles, then eyes me as she answers him, "I guess there's no other invitations," then her eyes drift to him, "so, sure. A girl has to eat."

"Nice meeting you, detective," I say. "Amber," and nod, then turn to leave.

"Thanks for the drink," she calls after me, and I wave over my shoulder. DiAngelo doesn't reply and I feel his eyes burn into my back as I head out.

It's time to check out Rosie's again and see if more trouble tries to climb on my back.

Chapter Four

The bikini-clad mannequin still rides the rocking horse oil pump sign outside of Rosie's, and the parking lot is already full. This time I don't have the problem of dragging a trailer and find a place nearer the front door. And this time the door's not half blocked by three simian throwbacks sucking down weed, and I push inside.

The place is jammed, and as before, the bar stools are covered with Carhartt clad butts and none of them female. This time it's Rascal Flatts booming out *Life is a Highway* so loud you have to read lips.

I elbow my way through the crowd and move to a barmaid's station to order a drink. There's a sport coat clad, balding guy leaning against the wall, arms crossed, looking a little like a bouncer, and he gives me a friendly nod as I move up. The old redhead is busy, but glances up and spots me, and I smile and nod...but she doesn't only come my way, she storms my way, and she's not smiling.

"You motherfucker," she spits, "you busted my kid's nose all to hell." The music is in changeover mode and the rest of the bar hears her, and like they are watching a tennis match, turn their heads to me, then back to her, then back to both of us as she stops just across the bar.

"That was your kid?" I ask.

"That was my kid, Emmitt, and you're not welcome around here. So get the fuck out."

I shrug and start to turn, but the guy who's leaning on the wall comes forward and puts a hand on my shoulder. "Hold on," he says, and not in an unfriendly way.

"I guess I've been eighty sixed," I say.

"Not yet. I own this joint, and I know Maggy's kids. What happened?" he asks.

"The one who got his nose broke was trying to cut a chain off my trailer, and I doubt if it was because he needed two feet of chain. His buddy was trying to pry the door open, so I encouraged them to leave my property alone."

He turns to the redhead, who's steaming. "That what Emmitt told you?"

She's so mad she's sputtering. "He told me this asshole blindsided him for no reason...and used a ball bat on him."

"For good reason," I offer, "and it wasn't a ball bat, it was a little ol' three eights of an inch baton," but she's not buying it.

"What are you drinking?" the bossman asks.

"Trout Slayer was good," I reply, and he nods at Maggy the bartender.

"Bullshit," she says, but turns and heads for the beer cooler.

"Thanks," I say to the boss, and extend my hand. "Dick Strong."

"Paul Feldman."

"Who's Rosie?" I ask with a tight grin.

"She fell through the ice on the river about twenty years ago. Never knew the lady," he says with a sly grin. "I bought it from her estate."

"Thanks for the beer," I say, and pick the one up that Maggy slams on the bar, hard enough that it foams out the neck.

"My pleasure," he says. "If those assholes give you any more trouble, let me know," he waves as he heads for a door marked 'office.'

"Will do," I call after him, but I won't, as I take care of my own problems.

I look for the hatchet-faced boy who, last night, made me the offer of damn near anything illegal but don't spot him. It's early yet, so maybe later. I shoot the bull with a couple of guys at the bar who are pipeline operator's for Allegany Petroleum, but learn nothing new as they seem to be hard-working guys who keep their noses clean, both of whom wish they were home with their families in Great Falls, Montana.

After downing my second beer, this one paid for out of my pocket, I decide to wander around the town and wait till later to give Rosie's another tumble, but have to hit the head first to get rid of some Trout Slayer. The johns are at the back of the place, down a hallway with a panic hardware exit door at the end.

I finish my business in the men's room, wash my hands, and head out. A big round-faced guy with black bangs and Indian features is leaning on the wall at the business end of the hallway, and looks as if he was waiting for me to leave before he hit the head, and starts my way as soon as I exit. From six feet away, his hand comes up and I get a glance of what appears to be wasp spray in his hand.

I don't quite get my eyes covered, when the spray hits me full in the face and takes both my breath and vision away. He drives into me, running me a dozen feet backwards, and we crash through the door into a snow bank in the rear parking lot.

Not able to catch my breath, I feel myself being hammered from all sides, go to my knees, trying to cover up I get off the snow bank and to the pavement and roll, but everywhere I go there's another blow from a pipe or two by four, there must be a half-dozen guys working me, until the lights go out.

Not out. Bright lights. Glaring lights. Not that I can open my eyes enough to see much. I reach up and feel my eyes and realized they're swollen badly, then pat around on my forehead and scalp, and find a dozen very sore spots, some of them now shaved bald and sporting the sharp ends of stitches under thin gauze.

Not many times in my life have I been suckered, but I'm feeling like one now, and it feels like crap. It hurts with every breath, and with every breath I get more pissed. I manage to open an eye enough to see that one of the walls of the room is glass, and people are moving about outside.

I try to lift my left arm, then move my right hand over to feel a splint on my left from elbow to hand.

"About time you came around," a voice emanates though the fog that's my blurry vision.

"Where am I?" I ask, then wince as my lips are split, top and bottom. I run my tongue around my mouth and am pleased to note that my teeth feel intact, but the stub of a stitch or two inside my swollen upper lip sticks my tongue. At least the odor of sweaty working men has been replaced by bleach and antiseptic.

"You're a guest of the Mercy Medical Center emergency room, and it's a good thing as you were about to freeze to death out there in the snow behind that terrible bar. You're lucky Mr. Feldman decided to have his swamper take a load of garbage out."

I manage to pry an eye open enough to see the face, and if I were feeling better, would be very pleased as she's a sandy haired angel, with eyes blue as my grandmother's hydrangeas. Had I seen her before I found out where I was, I'd of thought I was in heaven.

"And you're an angel of mercy?" I manage, and hear her pleasant laugh.

"I've been called worse," she says. "Stop flopping around. You've got an IV in your right wrist."

"Blood loss?" I ask.

"Hypothermia. Just replacing fluids and electrolytes. You'll be fine…now that you're awake."

"My wrist?"

"Slight break. You'll be wearing a cast for a while. What did you do to make somebody so mad? They beat the proverbial dog do do out of you."

"Must have been something I said," I answer, then add, "are you a married angel of mercy, or can I go home with you?"

"I get hustled about ten times a day in this berg, buster, but that's the first time from a guy who's been unconscious for a day and a half and just came to."

"You've got to be kidding. I've been out…"

"For a day and a half. And it's none of your business if I'm married or not. I've got to go get the doctor and let her know you've come around."

"I hope she's your sister...then again there couldn't be two like you." It pains me to talk, but she's worth the hurt.

Her laugh is pleasant as she exits the room. But not pleasant enough to make my head quit hurting. I feel like somebody dropped my camper on it.

It's only moments before another voice asks. "Can you tell me your name?"

There's not much sense in bullshitting as my Wyoming drivers license is in my wallet, and I'm sure the hospital has gone though it looking for my insurance cards.

"Mike...Mike Reardon." I pry an eye open to see a matronly salt-and-pepper haired woman in white smock bending over me, eyeing me over half-glasses.

"Good for you. You've got a concussion, you've been in a semi-coma, and I suspect some swelling of the brain. You're going to be with us a couple of days. Anyone we should call? I'm Doctor Samuelson by the way, and your nurse at the moment is Inga."

"Hi, ladies," I manage, letting my eye go shut again. "Nobody to call. Did my phone make it?"

"I don't know. Ask Inga to check for you. I'll be moving you into a room and out of the ICU. You've got enough scars for a ward full of small pox patients. Hard life?"

"Rough and tumble, most from Iraq."

"Well, I figured from the eagle, globe and anchor tattoo...the thanks for your service," she says, and I try to smile but it doesn't work well, and I wince instead.

"What time is it?" I ask.

"Almost noon. I'll try and get you upstairs before lunch is served."

"Soup, maybe."

"That we can do."

"Did those a-holes, pardon my language...did they steal my wallet?"

"Nope, all your ID is there, and you had eighteen nice fresh hundred dollar bills plus smaller stuff. Not that you'll have it when you leave, that is if you pay your way. Welcome to Mercy Medical. I'll check in with you before I leave today. How's the pain?" she asks, and I know she's leaving as her voice seems to come from the doorway.

"Better than the alternative," I say. "I hate drugs, so it's tolerable."

She laughs, and is gone.

I'll bet the old boy referred to as Emmitt, the redhead's kid, was one of the guys who met me with a pipe or baseball bat, and the Indian in the hallway, and God knows how many others, were the ones who put me in this hospital bed.

I guess they never heard the Biblical saying 'do unto others.'

I'm just the guy to teach it to them...but I've got to heal up first. But I'm going to teach them my version, 'Do unto others as they did to you, only worse. Sorry Jesus.

Chapter Five

Inga, with the ice blue eyes, brings me my personal belongings as soon as I'm rolled into my room. However, some things are missing. The room's not private, but the guy in the other bed is behind a drawn curtain. My first call is to Rosie's and Paul Feldman, its owner.

"Mr. Feldman," I ask, "as I know you know, as you were kind enough to call and get me a ride to the hospital, my pickup is still in your lot…unless you had it towed?"

He laughs. "Nope, I've been watching over it. Your doc will tell you I've been checking on you…really sorry that happened here at my place."

"Hell, I'm sorry it happened anywhere. Any idea who the boys were behind the bats?"

"Yeah, I've got an idea. Send the cops around and I'll fill them in."

"No, sir. No cops. I'll handle it myself when the time comes. Any idea where my Glock might be? It isn't with my things here."

"No idea…you were armed?"

"Yeah, but I don't advertise it and would appreciate it if you didn't. I'm permitted."

"The cops have already interviewed me," he says.

"And I'm sure they'll come have a chat with me, but I'll tell them nothing."

"Okay. You got a steak and a few beers coming whenever. Like I said, sorry that happened at my joint."

I no more than disconnect when a familiar, if not friendly, face leans in the door. "You got a clear head?" the detective I met at DiAngelo's, who's name is DiAngelo, is asking.

"Never claimed to have one, even before it was covered with knots."

He steps in without being invited. Again he's dressed immaculately, not for a dick from New York or San Francisco, but top end for North Dakota. He's in a brown-tone tweed jacket, a knit tie with brown and light blue, and a light blue shirt with dark blue monogramed initials on a sleeve. The jacket sports suede patches on the elbows. Perfectly creased Khaki colored slacks match one of the tones in the coat. Belt and Jodhpur boots match as if made from the same hide—even the tan leather holster clipped to his right side matches the belt. There's a thousand dollar camel overcoat draped over a forearm. He runs a splayed-fingered hand though his hair as he enters and his long shiny black hair falls exactly back into place, and drops the overcoat on a chair. The gray sideburns are a little too perfect and I suspect he spends more time in the beauty shop than any of the beautiful women I know. But that's just a guess.

He smiles and shows some expensive dental work, leans against the end of my bed and looks me up and down, then asks, "You slip on the ice or did you get the shit kicked out of you?"

I smile, purposefully a little sheepishly, "I got a face full of mace or wasp spray, got shoved through the back door, and that's the last I remember."

"Who was behind the spray can?"

"Big guy is all I know. Some Mongolian mother-fucker, pardon the expression."

"Not many Mongolian's around here, but lots of Indians. Who might have had it in for you?"

"Hell, I haven't been in town long enough to make any enemies."

"Oh, yeah. I heard there was a little scuffle in the front of the place a couple of nights ago, and you might have been involved?"

So I lie. "Not me. Night before last I had a beer and a sandwich and went home and curled up in my camper."

He shakes his head in doubt. "Not what I hear."

"That's how it was, detective."

"Where are you staying?"

I lie again. The last thing I want is for the cops to be nosing around my equipment trailer. "Here and there, wherever I can find a place to park for the night. Camper moves around, you know."

"Yeah, a patrolman's report says you got run out of the Ace Hardware parking lot a couple of nights ago. We frown on that around here."

"Okay, won't happen again. My first night in town and I didn't know the rules." I yawn as if I'm about to nod off, encouraging him to leave, but he doesn't so I ask, "If you hear anything about who was behind the bats, I'd sure like to know."

He looks a little more serious. "I don't think I have to tell you to leave this to us."

I lie even more earnestly, "Oh, God, no, I don't ever want to see those guys again. I just want to know who to stay away from."

He nods, but doesn't look convinced. Then asks, "You going to work for Owens-McKittrick?"

"That oil well service outfit—"

"Yeah, where you met my lady friend, Amber."

That comment rings of stay-the-fuck-away-from-my-girlfriend. But I skip right over it. "Nope, didn't get on there. They would have hired me as a roustabout for thirty bucks an hour, but I was looking for a security job."

He looks a little smug. "Yeah, I saw the concealed carry permit in your wallet, and the empty holster at the small of your back...but no weapon. You want to file a theft report?"

And admit I had a weapon in a bar, no way. "No, I just didn't bother to remove the holster before I went out. I thought I might eat someplace that served booze, so I left the PPK in my camper." I lie again, as my weapon was a Glock, not a Walther.

"Right," he says, but the look on his face says 'bullshit.' "So," he continues, but maybe my yawns are working as he's eyeballing the door, "you're not interested in filing charges? Walther is a nice weapon."

And not the one I lost. "Against who...a can of wasp spray and some Mongolian. I'm sure you've written a report."

"Oh, yeah, paperwork, the bane of all cops. But nothing will come of it."

"Such is life," I say, and yawn again.

"See you around, Reardon," he says, a little knowingly, and I'm sure he's run my record, not that there's much to find...if you don't count the guys I've shot in righteous shootings, and my general courts marshal from the Corps.

He heads for the door.

I call after him. "I'll probably be heading out of town when I get out of here."

He pauses in the doorway and gives me a very doubting look, then points an index finger at me and cocks his thumb with the other hand like he's bringing a police special to bear.

"I wouldn't discourage you...in fact, I'd think it might just be the smartest thing you've ever done," and he's gone.

My plaster has been replaced with a fiberglass cast, from just below the elbow to just behind my knuckles, with a roomy thumbhole. I'm studying it and thinking about how to do what my sweet mama always said, "when life hands you lemons, make lemonade," and I think I know just how to do that in this situation.

I'm in a full day and night before Doc Samuelson wanders in and gives me a quick exam then announces she's cutting me loose. I'm sorry to say Inga is off for the day, and I didn't get to pry her phone number out of her...as I've cajoled the fact she's a single girl out of the good doctor. This town is not so big that I won't see her somewhere.

I call the local cab company for a ride and am informed that it'll be an hour before they can get someone to Mercy Medical, so I call someone who may just be wanting to keep me in their good graces in this litigious world of ours. Paul Feldman, who owns Rosie's.

"Paul," I ask the girl who answers, and he comes on the line. "If you've got time, I need a lift back to your place to get my truck."

In ten minutes a fancy eighty grand Land Rover rolls up under the portico in front of the hospital.

Before I settle into the passenger seat, he offers, "I got a line on your friends."

"Good," I say and settle back for the ride to my rig. "I'll even let you off the hook for the steak and beer."

"No way, Jose. Just don't wipe the floor up with them in my joint."

"Not if I can help it. It'll be a while before that happens."

"By the looks of you, and that cast, it'll be at least six weeks."

I smile without looking over. "Don't count on it, my friend, don't count on it." Then I turn to him and ask, "you know a welder who's got some sculpting skills?"

"Strange request…but, yeah, I know a guy who lost a leg out in the patch and was a welder, now he makes a lot of goofy metal sculptures."

I laugh. "So you know a sculptor who knows how to weld. That'll probably do."

When we get back to Rosie's he offers me lunch and a beer—and gives me a list of five names of the guys who damn near beat me to death—but the hospital filled me up with a good breakfast so I pass, besides I want to find this guy Howie Dolittle, a sculptor who's name and address I've been given by Paul. As my cash has been drained by the hospital, I have to find an ATM, but do and am replenished with four hundred bucks. I punch the address into the computer in the Ford and it takes me out of town to a farmhouse in the middle of some fallow fields. There's smoke coming from a heater in a small red barn next to the house so I head there, and I pass some decent replicas of life size deer, elk, and bears on the way there.

I'm in debt to Paul as I have a to-do list in my pocket, and as I suspected, three of the names were the guys trying to break into my trailer. Real spoil sports...and real stupid, as they'll soon learn. Emmitt Radiston, Maggy's son; John Broken Toes; Albert Many Horses; Harold McAdams, also an Indian; and some guy whose name Feldman didn't know, but is a Russian who's only about five feet eight and weighs over two hundred and got a twisted right arm. He should be easy to find.

A bell rings loudly when I push the barn door open.

Howie is perched on a rolling stool, his single leg dangling, working on a life size crane and looks up, and pushes up his welding mask as I slip in and quickly close the door to try and keep the cold out. More critters of all sizes and shapes adorn the place, as well as a forge, a few propane tanks, and lots of raw metal.

"What can I do you out of?" he asks as I walk over and extend my right hand.

"A specialty job, if you're interested?" I ask.

Chapter Six

The metal sculptor doesn't look like your typical artist, but more like the oil patch welder he was before losing the leg a hand's width above the knee. In fact, by the size of his biceps, and strength of his grip, he more resembles an old blacksmith who bends iron for a living.

"Can't interest you in a life size whooper?" he asks with a smile, and nods his head toward the bird he's working on, which is just now getting its wings.

"No, sir. I've got some heavy work to do, and this is what I need." I begin explaining, and he listens intently.

In two hours I'm heading out of the metal menagerie for the truck, shy two hundred bucks. My fiberglass cast now has an exoskeleton, a one eighth inch thick, inch and a half wide strip of cold iron runs down both the back and underside of my forearm, over the fiberglass. It's formed into a ring around my hand and another just below the elbow. A half dozen three eights inch high nail-sharp spikes are welded across the back of the strip across my hand and across the palm side, and teed with a dozen down the strip on top and bottom of the arm. It's made in two pieces so it bolts together and can be removed. My wrist now is protected by the fiberglass, and doubly by the iron cage, and it's now more than just

43

a fair weapon. I'll have to remove it to get the cast off, but it's the price you have to pay. And my new buddy has made provision to get it on and off as it's in two halves and bolts together.

I feel a little like a knight right out of King Authur's court. Damn little, but a little.

As my sweet old mom would say, I've made lemonade out of the lemons I've been handed.

My first stop back in town is a Rite Aid where I pick up some gauze and wrap the whole forearm so the spikes are hidden in the depth of cotton gauze, then find a Boot Barn and pick up a couple of shirts, size XXL, that will fit nicely over the arm, although they are a little on the sloppy side otherwise.

Now to stay away from Rosie's for a few days and anywhere else where I might be tempted to test my new arm armor. The wrist needs a chance to set up, no matter the protection.

I shouldn't be rushing in where angels fear to tread anyway, so it's time to do some homework.

The Williston Community Library is an impressive structure across Davidson Road from some ballparks, tennis courts, and recreational buildings. I've come to the conclusion that Williston may be suffering from the boom, but it's also prospering. The town's a really nice blend of the historic and the new.

The girl behind the counter has plain black-rimmed glasses, cold black hair pulled into a bun, and a nicely mounded blouse buttoned high…but otherwise is not like the librarians I remember, with piercing ebony eyes and just enough bright red lipstick. I'd bet a ten dollar bill against a donut that she has a pair of bright red come-fuck-me five inch heels in her closet and does most of her reading in the romance section. She's all business however, I'm sorry to say, as she directs me to the newspapers and a computer that will allow me to dig into those digitized, not ones still on file in paper format. I can understand her reluctance to strike up a conversation as I look a little like a refugee from a recent gang war.

The digital variety is fine as I like the computer better as the search feature takes me directly to the subject at hand...dope and prostitution.

So I bear down on the task at hand.

I work for a couple of hours, investing twelve bucks in print copies, then head back to check on the camper and Wells Cargo trailer. Even though it's double locked, I still worry like hell as there are implements inside that could get me hard time, and hard time in a place as friggin' cold as North Dakota would be ice hard.

The trailer's still there and still locked up tight, and the camper is fine, except the water line is frozen up—I have to get my head back into cold weather mode. I make a phone call to get some plane reservations, grab some clean clothes, pack a small carry on duffle, and head out to find a gym where I can shower and change.

I'm feeling a little paranoid about my stuff as one of the Bakken's major problems is theft. I've been following one of the fastest growing pages on facebook, The Fail of the Day, which has lots of Bakken info on a daily basis—mostly about wrecks on the highway and in the fields—and reports a stolen trailer almost daily, and sometimes more than one. They also have missing people reported, mostly women, some of whom have not been found.

Since every bone in my body aches just slightly less than every joint, and each of those feel like a nail's been hammered in between the bones, and since damn near every bad guy in the county now knows my F250, I decide it's a good time to regroup. It'll be at least a week before I'm close to fighting shape, if then, and then I'll have to be careful who and how I challenge.

So I've scheduled a flight out of Bismark back to Vegas to take care of biz, heal up, and study up on the Bakken and the dope problem. And since I have no interest in leaving my truck in an airport parking lot then having to go way out of my way to pick it up, as I'll be driving another rig back to Williston, I decide to ride the dog over to the capitol, and cab it to the bus station. Greyhound to the state capitol is a little over a four-hour ride, but it'll give me a chance to read some of the ream of stuff I've copied while doing my research at the library. And I've got a ream of crap to read.

During my last self-imposed assignment—a brand new client got murdered and I took it upon myself to revenge the lady—one of my three vehicles got badly cratered, and it was the center of operations for me. But it's been repaired and refitted and awaits me in my Vegas ministorage, thanks to my buddy Pax Weatherwax taking care of business for me in my absence. My absence involved a sailboat trip to the Cayman Islands where I deposited a duffle bag full of cash that I'd relieved from a drug cartel, as a number of their members no longer needed same, unless cash is the form of exchange in hades. I brought the dough back into the country via bank transfers and, like the good citizen I try to be, will claim it on my tax return as consulting fees.

My Dodge Van served as camouflage on many a job; and as home from time to time with its fold down cot, sink with instantaneous hot water, and even a porta-potty, the throw away bag kind. But those aren't its most valuable assets. It has an abundance of hide out storage—most in the side panels but some in ceiling and floor—several license plates, a variety of magnetic signs and magnetic color striping, which allows me to appear to be a local plumber, a landscaper, a pizza delivery man, and even a swat vehicle as I carry magnetic red lights as well. And it also contains personal disguise accouterments including coveralls to match the signs, and thanks to an old buddy who's now a Hollywood guru, facial disguise. And, of course, a variety of weapons are well hidden inside wall panels and in a hollow floor compartment.

And she's not only four wheel drive, lifted for extra clearance in tough country, but Hemi powered and can dust most pursuit vehicles.

The Marine Corps taught me that having the right equipment was the difference between winning and losing, living and dying.

Speaking of equipment, I have to unbolt my new armor from my arm, pack it in a small bag which I'll check, as it would be frowned upon by the boys and girls at the airport should I try to board with it in place. Which is fine as I doubt if I'll be in any jousts on my trip down.

I call my buddy Pax from the Denver airport, email him the picture I took of the guys at the bar who tried to line me up with a fifteen year old, beg a ride from McCarran and ask him to get us a date for dinner, hopefully with a young lady who had to fall by the wayside while I was involved in my last confrontation with bad guys. She was my one regret from a week's endeavors. Jennifer DiMarco is her name, Keno running her game, and I doubt seriously if Pax has any luck, as she thinks I'm a major smuck. There may be a song in there somewhere.

But it's worth a try as it's been a little over two months since I twice stood her up…and hated doing so, but duty calls. It's twice as bad when you stand a beautiful woman up after enjoying a highly satisfying roll in the hay with her, and truly looking forward to a rematch.

My buddy Paxton Weatherwax was a fellow Desert Storm Marine, who saved my bacon more than once, and the last time he did so he lost an inch and a half out of his left thigh thanks to an AK47. Still, even with a platform shoe, I'd take him as a back up before ninety nine point nine percent of the supposedly tough guys I've come across. And Pax is not only double tough, but triple smart. He's turned his disability pay into a business as an internet service provider with offices in four cities. He's kept me out of the all-seeing-eye of the fed for several years, routed my dough and messages through a half dozen cities in as many countries, and dug up information needed in my dubious endeavors and the on subjects of my attentions—wrath normally being the attention paid them—to rival the NSA. And he's more than just a buddy, as I'd get between him and a Cruise Missile should it come to that.

Chapter Seven

The pile of newspaper clippings I've printed are very enlightening. For one thing, I gain new respect for Detective Antonio DiAngelo, who it turns out has had two major shootouts with drug runners and who singlehandedly chased a van full of human traffickers over the border into Canada where they were promptly apprehended by the Mounties, with him still hot on their tails.

So, he's not just a pretty face under a fancy hairdo. I'll have to pay him a little more respect.

The flight to Vegas is uneventful, except for a very rough landing in Denver and a two hour layover.

Pax, like the good buddy he is, waits at the curb in his second car, a CJ7, for me to recover my bag and load up.

He sees me exit the building and his expression changes from smile to grimace as I near the vehicle, then he calls out, "What the fuck, over?" When I merely give him a grimace in return, he adds, "you look like one of those Bakken field oil rigs fell on you."

"Five or six assholes with bats and pipes fell on me, after they shot a little wasp spray in my puss."

He shakes his head and mumbles, "Just can't let the boy go out into the world without his buddy Pax."

"Trust me," I manage, as I fling a duffle in the back, "I wish you'd have been there. I busted three of them up pretty good a couple of nights before they nailed me...and I should have seen it coming, but I'd just walked out of the john in a bar when they hit me with the spray...and that crap makes you lose it fast."

"Guess what?" he asks as I pile in the Jeep.

"I'm guessed out," I say, and yawn.

"Babs has convinced Miss Jennifer to join us...which I imagine is just so she can chastise your ugly butt for standing her up so many times."

"Hell, I'll take an ass chewing from her anytime...so long as we end the night bosom buddies. And it's great bosoms she has."

"She'll take one look at your beat and bruised butt and run for the hills. What's with the cast on the wrist?"

"Broken, but not bad. Just a crack."

"To bad they didn't hit you just on your granite-hard head, which I see they did plenty of. But on to more important things than you getting your butt whipped. So, guess what else?"

"Amaze me even more."

He talks as he works the Jeep out into traffic, and guns it. "I got a file full of stuff on Travis Richter Speck, the guy whose pic you emailed me, and on a bunch of his cohorts. He's a bad apple, but he won't spoil the barrel, as all his buddies are as bad or worse. You got yourself into a den of snakes this time."

I nod knowingly, but actually don't know ka ka yet. "Well, I'm not 'in' yet. But I plan to get in. You got pics on these guys?"

"Two of them are right off the Rez. Big Indian boys."

"Yeah, I met them, I'm sure."

"Mandan or Arikara, one of them is Big John Broken Toes and the other is Albert Many Horses. Both did a nickel in the state pen for assault and each of them has been busted for possession, but not enough to put them away for the duration. And there's a half dozen more scumbags in the mix including some just-as-soon-kill-you-as-look-at-you Russians who've been running girls down from Canada."

"Yeah, I got a lot of it from the local library. It's been bad all over the Bakken, and is getting nothing but worse."

"You're going to need an army up there."

I laugh. "I don't plan to solve the problem in Montana, North Dakota, and Canada. I'm being paid to solve the problem at Owens-McKittrick Oil Well Service."

"Good luck," he says and in minutes we're pulling up at the rear of his two story office building.

I walk to the front of the office before going upstairs so I can give Pax's rotund little receptionist a hug.

"Rosie," I call out, and she jumps up and flings her arms around me, "hey, you'll never guess what my favorite new hangout in North Dakota is named," I semi whisper in her ear.

She plants a slobbery kiss on my cheek then holds me at arm length and asks, "The Pussy Galore lounge?"

"Very funny. Nope, it's Big Rosie's."

"I could understand sweet little Rosie's," she says.

"Close as I could get to something that reminds me of my favorite girl."

"A classy place, I'm sure," she says with a typical Rosie giggle.

"I cannot tell a lie, it's a dump but that's not the part that reminds me of you," I say with a laugh.

"Better not be."

I wave over my shoulder as I head up the stairs to Pax's office.

When I walk in he's smiling. "What's with the Cheshire cat grin?" I ask.

"I found a couple of warrants out on your boy Speck, and he skipped bail from some bondsman…," he glances back at the file, "Bail Bond Bender, down in Galveston."

"Never heard of them, but I'll call—"

"I already emailed them in your name and success record, said you had a lead, and asked for a contract. It's only fifty grand bail, but what the hell, twenty percent is ten grand and ten grand is ten grand if this guy Bender goes for it."

"I can't imagine he wouldn't, and it'll be a nice lever to have should I need to put a little pressure on Speck."

I carry a bail enforcement officer's badge, but that's not really my vocation although it comes in handy and on seldom occasion results in a few bucks. A bounty hunter needs a contract from a bondsman in order to do his thing.

"We'll see if a contract comes back." Pax is still grinning. "Now to more important biz…the gorgeous blond Jennifer has agreed to give you a chance to redeem yourself."

Now it's my turn to grin. "So, we got a dinner date?"

"Late dinner, she's working until ten."

"Cool, I've got to go pick up the van and reload it from the mini-storage, so I can keep busy. Can I meet you at your place about eight so I can shower and change."

"See you there. I've got some work so I'll have Sol drive you over." He digs in a desk drawer and fishes out a key and throws it to me with, "I had to buy a new lock for the unit the van's in...number two sixty four."

"I can cab it."

"Fuck you, Farley." He reaches for his desk phone and it's an intercom and in seconds his pudgy little office computer guru is at the door, smiling and jumping up and down like he'd just won the lottery. His sweatshirt says, *Internet Experts Delve Deeper*, which makes me smile.

"Hi, big Mike," he says. "Let's go."

As I'm heading for the door, Pax calls after me, "By the way, I tracked down an email account for Specter, and found his computer. Looks like he's out to the west of Williston a few miles. He's got a typical lousy firewall and we'll have a Trojan Horse in it soon...won't we, Sol," he yells.

"Yes, sir," Sol yells back as we descend the stairs.

Sol drives a Prius, bright red with every gadget known to man, and is a real groupie when it comes to the rougher side of my biz. He's always picking my brain about what happened and where, but generally all I'll talk about is my time in the Corps...but he knows a lot of what I've done as he's done much of the background work digging info out of the internet, and in fact placed a Trojan Horse in the computer of some cartel guys on my last case, a dozen of whom took a painful trip to Hades. Pax, himself does the real critical stuff, but Sol can't help but be curious when he's done research on some criminal cat who turns up, toes up, or at least in the headlines for being busted, as he knows it's too much of a coincidence. It's always a righteous act—at least most often—on my part, but Sol has no way of knowing that, except for the fact I'm not doing twenty-five to life in some gray-stone mansion.

I no more than get my seatbelt hooked up in the little electric monster when he starts with the inquisition, which I knew was coming.

"So, that big shootout down in California was you and Pax…and that other guy…Skip was his name?"

I laugh. "What shootout?"

"You know what shootout. Why won't you guys ever level with me?"

"You don't want to know. If we tell you we'd have to bury you in the desert." I'm kidding, but he blanches and his lips go tight as a lizard.

"Sorry…," he mumbles, and keeps his eyes on the road.

I laugh. "Sol, you're Pax's most valuable employee and you know it. Sometimes it's better not to know stuff. You're the number one guy around Weatherwax Internet Services and Pax can't do without you." I pause for effect. "I sure as hell can't."

This brings the grin back to his face.

I'm glad to reach the mini-storage as he's started back on Iraq, which he knows I'm somewhat willing to talk about, but to be truthful, there are lots of memories I'd rather leave buried. I jump out of the Prius at the gate in mid-sentence and give him a wave and head in through the walk-in gate, having to poke in the code first.

Pax has rented a van size unit for the vehicle and has been lucky enough to rent one next to one I already had where my prize possession is garaged. My classic Vette.... The 1957 Corvette I keep stored there is, of course, a rarity. Red with white inserts, it's absolutely original...except for the blown, tricked out engine—requiring a scoop breather in the hood—the racing transmission and rear end, and a roll bar I added knowing my propensity to overdo things...I've flipped more than one vehicle. With racing slicks it's good for a hundred forty or more in the quarter mile, if I put slicks on the back, and top end is beyond my reckoning. There's not much room in the trunk of a Vette, so I've left the chrome luggage rack in place over the trunk lid.

I seldom take her into harms way, as I value her way too much. She's my pride and joy.

The van is primo again. I'd folded in the front of it with a pursuit and the body shop has done a great job with both the repair and paint. And it starts I'm happy to learn. I idle it out, close the unit, and move a couple of rows over to my primary unit which contains my life history, and several items so I'll continue to have a history.

I maintain mini-storage spaces in three cities: Las Vegas, Nevada; Ventura, California and Sheraton, Wyoming. And they are not just for storing my old high school pictures and the antique clock grandma left me. In addition to the bug-out bag I keep in the van, which can now go back in, there's enough weaponry to start a revolution in most third world countries.

With any of the major bug-out bags I have in each mini-storage unit, and a mini-version I keep in the bags on the back of my Harley Sportster. I could live in the Rockies, the Sierras, or the deserts for a long, long time, if not forever, without the benefit of cities, if you can call cities a benefit.

I've accumulated a nice collection of weapons, which will again be widely distributed among secret side panels in the van, and in hideouts in the three storage rooms. On casual observation, you see no weapons. In each storage room I have an upright armoire size cabinet with hidden weapon storage. Both ends swing open with hidden push latches to reveal four long arms in each, and drawers inside what appear to be three inch thick shelving, which hold ammunition, side arms, and other accouterments. The shelves are covered with clothes and other mundane items to make the armoire look as if that's its purpose.

My Vegas unit is on a major thoroughfare, Tropicana, right on the edge of the action. These days most modern ministorage facilities have sophisticated computer entrance monitors which record your entrance-exit, and consequently are not a place to hide out or even spend the night, unless you're adept at scaling the eight foot fences and dodging cameras, and even then some are monitored with motion alarms. The Tropicana is such a facility, so I never bunk there…besides, the van has a fold down cot and tiny sink and port-a-potty, all the conveniences of home. And almost every truck-stop or highway rest-stop will do for a free overnight…not that I'm too cheap to pay, but paying means registering, and registering means leaving tracks, even if with phony personal identification and a plethora of plates.

You can't stay under the radar if you leave tracks.

But I do plan to leave tracks, across the backs of some North Dakota Bakken oil field dope dealers. But not until I heal up a little, and have the chance to be, hopefully, pampered by a beautiful blond.

And that's on top my list, after I restock the van.

Chapter Eight

Most of my bag of tricks are already in Williston in the Wells Cargo trailer I towed up. But there are a few more weapons I might as well haul as I'm taking the van, and it has hide-out panels in the walls and floor that will accommodate same. As they could have been traced, if not through ownership through ballistics, to a few I owned during our last major shoot out where Pax, Skip—another Marine Corps buddy—and I engaged in a major battle with some cartel misfits, many of my firearms were deep-sixed into the Hoover Dam end of Lake Mead.

One of those weapons now over four hundred feet deep in Mead was a XM110 SASR, a semi-auto sniper rifle in .308 caliber and was my baby, but thank God Pax was able to pick up another one on the black market, and I plan to find a lonely spot on the way back to Williston to make sure it's dead on. It has a removable scope and a night vision scope as part of the package, but it should have for the six and a half grand he laid out, which will require my reimbursement as soon as I dig the cash out of the hideout safe in my mini-storage.

I spend a couple of hours leisurely digging around in my stuff and reloading the van before I find some decent threads to wear to dinner tonight, then lock things up.

In khaki slacks, a light blue dress shirt that I could barely get over my cast, a dark blue blazer, brown leather belt and loafers—the only pair of dressy shoes I own—I wander down Pax's stairway from the guest room in his condo, to find his current live-in lady, Babs. And I say current as I claim he's had more than a dozen even though he claims only a couple.

She's mixing some concoction at his bar.

She glances up and gives me a questioning smile. "Hey, big boy, you clean up pretty good if it weren't for the bruises and bumps." She laughs out loud, then adds, "And the shaved patch on your head and stitches don't add much. You're not shaving your ugly mug?"

"Nope, going all out with the beard and stash…. The rest is the best I could do."

"I'll reserve my opinion. You want a Manhattan?"

"No, thanks. I'd go for a beer."

She reaches under the bar to its built-in fridge and comes up with a bottle of some microbrew and pops the cap with a church-key and hands it over as I reach the bar and mount a stool.

"You're a gentle-lady," I say, and toast her before taking a drink.

She smiles again and shakes her head. "And you're six kinds of a jerk. You know Jennifer really likes you, even though you did stand her up a half dozen—"

"Twice," I correct, "and it was life or death or it wouldn't have happened."

Again she shakes her head then adds with a serious gaze, "Try and treat my best friend a little better…she deserves it."

"I'm glad she's giving me the chance to treat her better."

"We'll see," she says, then glances over where Pax, in his stocking feet, is limping down the stairs.

I'm so used to seeing my buddy in shoes or boots that have an elevated sole on his short-leg side so he walks normally, and it kind of surprises me.

He notices me watching him, looks up and says very graciously, "Fuck you, Reardon."

I laugh and offer, "Had you not given up a chunk of that leg we'd both be looking up at the sod."

He laughs in return, finally hits the floor, and growls at me, "I often wonder if you were worth the effort."

"No more than I do, old buddy. Want a beer?"

"My darling is making me a Manhattan, thanks anyway."

He joins us at the bar just as the doorbell rings. I take a quick look at my phone, checking the time and see it's only ten fifteen. She didn't waste any time. I hope that's good news. "I'll get it," I say, and jump up a little too eagerly.

I open the door and we stand looking at each other for a moment, then she brushes by without a peep and heads for the bar.

"Hi," I call after her.

She turns, walks back, doubles up a fist, and busts me in the shoulder; a pretty good shot for a small woman, and as sore as I am, I wince.

"Oh," she says, looking surprised, "did I really hurt you?"

"Severely…you bruised my fragile ego," I say, and laugh.

"Good, I'm happy now. I do have a little trouble believing that your ego can be bruised, however I'll shine that one on. Let's start over?"

"Absolutely my pleasure."

She reaches up and caresses my cheek. "You going for the four day beard Hollywood look…trying to prove you've got some testosterone?"

"Nope, going for the real beard and mustache thing."

She shrugs nonchalantly, then says as she turns, "Everybody's got to be somewhere and somebody. With all the knots and stitches, it looks like you're going for a Frankenstein look."

I smile, as she's close to right. "Good thing you're hot for rugged looking men."

"Good thing," she says, and giggles.

Jennifer heads to the bar, and Babs hands her a Manhattan, and it's as if those to failures-to-appear on my part never happened.

We have a couple more drinks with dinner—a great steak at Cut, a Wolfgang Puck steakhouse—which turns out to be a super supper with lots of laughs, and I follow her lead and a half hour after my dessert, am in her apartment having her for my second and much more delicious dessert. As good as Puck's dessert was, my second was five star and possibly irreplaceable. Thank goodness she has a Jacuzzi, as after an hour rolling in the hay, I need my bones and joints massaged. I still hurt in spots I didn't know I had until those Williston misfits took me apart at the seams…but somehow I've forgotten those aches and pains for a while.

I awake to her arousing my interest again, and a second bout, which I finally concede to her as the flat out winner as I'm not only sore from the Williston misfits but from her very athletic performance—I get the distinct impression she wants to make sure I show up on time for any subsequent dates, and I can't imagine ever being late again, much less not showing.

After a half hour in her steaming shower I'm beginning to feel human again, so I dress—except I can't find the V-neck tee shirt I had on last night, and join her in her little kitchen, where an omelet is almost complete.

I've found the V-neck, which looks much better on her, particularly when that's all she's wearing. My cleavage never looked quite that good.

"What's up today?" she asks. "I don't have to be at work until two."

"I'm off to the beauty shop," I say, and can't help but grin.

That stops her short and she turns and eyeballs me. "If you're gay you put up one hell of a false front."

That makes me laugh aloud, then ask, "How do you think I'd look as a blond?"

She shakes her head. "With all that hair on your chest and back, it'll take a gallon of peroxide to convince anyone."

"I've only got to convince a bunch of old boys in a very dark saloon. I've got to head back to North Dakota and have a chat with the boys who gave me this cast…and I don't want them to see me coming. And I've got work to do there…work that may require me to be someone other than Mike Reardon for a while."

"It'll be pretty hard to hide those stitches in your scalp—"

"Come on, you've heard of a wig."

"And those knots on your cheek bones, and that black eye."

"They'll be gone before I get back there, as I have to wait at least a week to get this arm in shape."

"I'll dye it for you if you want. That military stubble on your head won't take much."

"You're too sweet, but I've got a friend in the beauty biz. You know Beauty by Crystal?"

"Sure, had a pedicure there last year."

"Can you drop me off there?" I ask. "I need to check on her anyway."

She stops on the way to the table, a plate of eggs and sausage in each hand, and eyes me suspiciously. "If I'm not going to see you again, this plate is going straight into the garbage."

"No, no, that's not what I meant. But I do want to pick up my van at Pax's office, then I'll meet you wherever, whenever. You're not going to get rid of me that easily."

She moves on to the table, plops a plate on either side, goes back to her Mr. Coffee and pours me a cup, picking up a couple of slices out of the toaster on the way back.

"Crystal's it is," she says.

Crystal Janson was the twin sister of Carol Janson, who hired me just before she was murdered by the cartel in order to convince her husband not to turn state's evidence. Her killing set off a series of events that left bodies strewn around Nevada and California. I'd been hired to find Carol's daughter after the husband absconded with her. As fate would have it, some smart attorney held off on the husband's agreement arguing for better terms with the Federal Marshal's Service, so when the subject of his testimony, a pair of Vegas mobbed up brothers, were killed, the Fed reneged as the agreement had not been signed, and he went to the pen for violating the RICO act. The daughter, luckily, ended up with her aunt...Crystal. Unknown to the authorities, we made off with a little expense money, a couple of satchels full even though we left a couple of satchels full, after a gun battle with the cartel, and set up a trust with a chunk of it for the daughter, little Sherry.

I called and made an appointment to have my hair dyed, and luckily, Crystal was in when I arrived. She was, to say the least, surprised when I knocked on her office door.

"I thought you were sailing the Caribbean?" she said, as she threw herself into my arms. She was equally beautiful, obviously as an identical twin of her departed sister. But she was off limits to me as every time I saw Crystal I pictured her sister, sans her beautiful head, as the cartel left her.

"I was, for months, but I'm back. I'm working up north and need a hair job, so here I am."

"Doesn't compute," she said as she turned to her desk and motioned to me to take a chair across from hers.

"A little disguise is in order."

She sighs deeply, smiles, and shakes her head. "You are beyond belief."

"Believe me, I need to change my looks."

She laughs again and says, "It looks like somebody has already tried to change them. Or did you get hit by a train?"

"Nope, just a trainload of bad guys. Who can give me a dye job and fix me up with a matching dirty blond wig?"

She's on her feet and circling the desk, waving me up. "I'll do it myself. We don't get much request for 'dirty blond.' Sexy satin blond won't do?"

"Nope, as close to looking like a homeless person as you can get me…eyebrows, chest hair, arm hair and all, and some way to keep it that way for a while."

"Let's go to work."

We talk about little Sherry as she works, and I am proud of the work that Skip, Pax and I did that resulted in the little girl becoming a ward of her aunt. She gives me a ride back to Pax's condo, where I've left my van. I leave with a kindergarten picture of Sherry in my wallet, my head, body, and facial hair blond…and supplies and instructions as to how to stay blond. And I leave with stringy blond hair to my shoulders, thanks to a wig they had to rework. Had it not been for the fact I still have on my light blue dress shirt, I would look exactly like a dumpster diver. I'll make a transition the rest of the way to 'homeless' or at least dirty Hell's Angel type before I get back to Williston.

The good news is I won't have to wear the itchy damn wig until I cross the North Dakota border.

For the next several days I spend the late nights and mornings with Jennifer, the late mornings working out at Gold's and running on the University of Nevada track putting down five miles jogging, the afternoons working with Pax, and do some serious 'rest up and heal.'

On the Thursday before I leave I ask, "If I'm Frankenstein, how about you being nurse Crachet?"

"I forgot to go to nursing school," she says, and eyes me a little suspiciously.

"Okay, did mama teach you to sew?"

"Yeah, a little."

"Then get your tiniest scissors. I need these stitches out."

"Oh, that gives me the willies."

"You can do it. It's no hill for a stepper."

"Can I do it with my eyes closed?"

"You only have to do the ones on the back of my noggin. I can do the ones I can see."

In less than ten minutes, I'm unstitched.

It is early on a rainy Friday morning when I say goodbye to the beautiful keno runner.

She hauls my ashes like they've never been hauled before, something to remember her by, then we depart her king size bed. She fixes me a great breakfast after I've showered and dressed, then follows me out to the van. After a long clinging hug, she asks, "Well, Mr. Reardon, will I ever see you again?"

"God willin' and the creek don't rise," I answer, as I climb behind the wheel.

"Seriously?" she asks.

"I'll be back, and when I get back, you'll be the first to know."

"I wonder…."

I start the van, and give her a wink. "I always do what I say I'll do, darling. If I don't, you can count on me being cold and on a slab."

She slaps me on my left arm, hard enough that it stings. "Don't you say that. I'm counting on you coming back, whole."

I reach out and hook a left hand behind her neck and drag her over for one more deep kiss, then gently push her back.

"See you soon, Jen Jen."

And I'm off to clean up the Bakken oil field, at least the Owens-McKittrick Oil Well Service part of it.

Chapter Nine

I've got a thumb drive in my glove compartment with not only dossiers on half the bad guys operating in North Dakota and eastern Montana, but with pictures, mostly mug shots. I also have a keystroke register, thanks to Sol's Trojan Horse being planted in Travis Richter Speck's computer. You can trace everything done on his computer with the keystroke register and with another program, convert those keystrokes to text. Pax has discovered that Speck owns an Apple laptop, and iPod, and an iPhone, all of which he has foolishly turned on the "find my…" feature, which allows you to search on another device for that device if lost. We now know where he lives, works, and travels, as we can track him thanks to him not trusting those who might steal from him, or himself as to where he might leave his electronics inadvertently.

I make it all the way to Billings before I whip into a truck stop and find a spot to park for the night, and to feed my face. I barely step out of the van before I'm met by a hooker in purple hot pants over yellow tights. She's a redhead, or so she wants folks to think...actually in the yellow no-bug lights of the parking lot, it looks more Sunkist orange than red. And she's wearing yellow lipstick. Few black girls are natural redheads, and to be truthful, it's all I can do not to break out laughing.

"You lookin' for a good time," she asks, giving me a wink. She's got that dislocated look of one who's riding the white horse, but her eyes are not wholly dilated so she's not completely out of it.

"If I was, you'd be the one," I lie, and return the wink as I lock up the van, and as an extra precaution, check the back doors which are facing away from the restaurant and thus out of sight. I have them barred from the inside, so it's overkill. You'd have to have a cutting torch to get through them.

"One thin Ben, and you'll have the ride of your life, big boy." She bats her big brown eyes at me coyly. She is cute, for a truck stop hooker.

I laugh. "Why aren't you working the Bakken like half the girls north of Texas."

She gets serious. "I was up there for a while, I was a boomtown girl, but them boys is too damn mean for this Louisiana girl. You know what I'm saying?"

"Nope, I don't. Walk with me," I say, heading for the restaurant.

"Sure, I gots to pee anyway. And there ain't no spenders around no how."

"So, the customers up there around the Bakken are too damn mean?"

"Nope, the Johns is fine, the family mans are."

"One more time."

"The pimps, they all mean as pit bulls to all we wifies. Them communist cocksuckers are bad, bad, bad, you knows what I mean?"

"The Russians don't appreciate hard working capitalists—"

69

"What's dat?"

"Hard working enterprising working girls like you. Have you had dinner?" I ask, as I hate to eat alone and may learn something from this hard working young lady.

"Why, you don't think your gonna trade no cheap hamburger for some sweet meat—"

I laugh and interrupt her. "No, ma'am. I'm thinking you might be hungry and I hate to eat alone."

She studies me for a minute as if she can't believe I'm only offering to buy her supper.

So I add, "Hells bells, girl, you been turning tricks so long you don't recognize a nice guy when you see one?"

"Sure 'nuf, but I be wanting a steak, you knows what I mean?"

"I do know what you mean, and if you're having a steak, so am I, and I'm buying. We gonna live it up."

She hooks an arm through mine, tells me her name is Vanna White, which makes me smile as it's quite a stretch from the Vanna I know from TV to the one I now know in this snow-covered truck stop parking lot.

I'm allowed to escort the lovely, and colorful, Vanna inside. The receptionist looks at me like a bull at a bastard calf, but picks up a couple of menus and escorts us to the back of the restaurant, as far as she can get from the door and other customers.

Vanna's not bashful and orders a porterhouse and twice baked, the most expensive meal on the menu, but in this joint that only means twenty nine ninety five, plus a drink and a tip. I can handle it and order the same, but hers is well done and mine medium rare, but still tough as a Cajun cage fighter who grew up wrestling alligators for sport. It's Gold's Gym for the jaw.

In the bright light of the coffee shop I see the make up covering the needle tracks on her arms.

I innocently lay my iPhone on the table between us, after activating the audio record app so I won't forget anything she might say of value.

I don't leave the place with much, other than a couple of places where the girls hang, and the nicknames of four different Russian pimps. The Bear, who she thinks is a guy named Bogdan, who should be easy to find as she says he's over four hundred pounds and walks with a limp due to bad knees, and is white haired with ice blue watery eyes; Vasily, who's nicknamed V-One; another she thinks is Victor, who's nicknamed V-Two; and Alexei, who's called Luthor on the street, I presume a play on Batman's Lex Luthor. He'll be easy to spot as she says he's missing the lobe of one ear and the stub has the rough edge of teeth marks. The two V boys are average height, but muscled up like no-neck gym rats, and Luthor is over six feet tall, but thin and sallow cheeked with a Van Dyke goatee. With her names and descriptions, added to what I imagine are Russian accents, they shouldn't be hard to find. When questioned about dope, she acts as if it's matter of fact that all of them are selling meth, crack, and Mexican brown.

She says she's trying to earn enough dough to get back to New Orleans, and wants to head for the bus station as soon as she earns another hundred...back to where mama lives and where she wants to go back to college. I was born at night, but not last night, but I give her a thin Ben none-the-less as I'm an undying optimist.

And, undoubtedly, a sucker. She offers to do me a solid in the form of a quick blowjob, but I shake hands with her instead and wish her a good trip. Then being not quite so much a sucker use Peril to sanitize my hands.

I roll back into Williston with the temperature at ten degrees, but no snow and only a high overcast and whisper of wind. I've been gone an even two weeks and am feeling strong.

When I drive out at dawn, The girl who calls herself Vanna White is leaning into the window of a Kensworth with a load of bawling cattle on the back.

So much for a college education.

I've been lucky so far, but as soon as I head northeast out of Billings on I-94 the weather hits, and it's blowing snow horizontal for an hour, then slows down to just making snow snakes on the highway. Wiggling lines of snow move like the highway's covered with hyper white pythons, and they are dangerously mesmerizing and hypnotizing.

Then the wind picks back up and I only make it a couple of hours before I get off the highway, believing the roadside signs with great faith as I can't see over thirty yards into the mess, and only pray there's a coffee shop, and it's open. But the sign is not lying and there's a café with windows so dirty you can hardly see inside or read the shimmering neon beer signs trying to attract through the muck, but with great pie if lousy coffee, and, shock of shocks, free Wi-Fi. I kill two hours and a piece of lemon meringue, which is so good I top it off after a couple of cups of float-a-spoon bitter coffee with Apple a la mode. I spot a chunky Hispanic lady with double chins working the kitchen and am sure the crust is so melt-in-the-mouth good because it's made with real lard. There go the arteries.

The good news is I'll still make Williston in time for a late lunch, not that I'll be hungry. But I plan to visit DiAngelo's and see if the blond disguise is working.

Disguise is not only changing your hair color and dress, but as important is how you walk, talk, and your general demeanor. I have a tendency to look people straight in the eye in a manner some find almost challenging. Now I'll have trouble meeting someone's gaze and will keep my eyes down. I'll change the temblor of my voice and the pacing of my speech. I also have a pair of dark glasses that a buddy in Hollywood has furnished. They have prosthetic devices that flare your ears out, and flat ears become Dumbo ones. I have inserts for my cheeks that fatten them. I've fooled facial recognition software more than once with these little additions, particularly when I add phony paste on eyebrows and a mustache or beard...or both. Now my beard and stash is over a quarter of an inch, and blond, and my eyebrows are died blond, so I don't need paste-ons. My eyes are brown, but contacts, which I very seldom wear, change them to a spooky dark, dark blue with gold accents. I don't bother with them.

I drive straight to my new residence—the truck, camper, and Wells Cargo trailer—and am relieved to see my vehicles are still as I left them, including the water being frozen up on the camper. I pull a bale of straw aside and place my electric heater under the camper, replace the bale, and hope that by the time I'm back from testing my disguise, the pipes will be thawed out.

I spend a half hour in front of the little mirror in the camper, and leave a different guy. I'm wearing well-worn Marine camo pants, a leather flight jacket that's skinned and frayed at the cuffs and knit collar, a gray turtle neck knit sweater that's been obviously re-woven in spots, and phony Ugg snow boots that are stained and matted with tar. My hat is one of those with the fold-down fur lined ear covers, and my stringy blond wig flares out from under it to my shoulders. I wear the glasses that flare my Dumbo ears and use the inserts in my cheek. It's a good thing I'm not hungry as it's hard to eat with the cheek inserts, so I'll try the soup.

I decide to leave my new armor off the broken wrist as DiAngelo's, at lunch, is not a trouble spot...in fact, I doubt if it's one at two A.M. closing time.

There's a tire shop a half block from DiAngelo's so I open the Wells Cargo and unload my Harley, lock things back up tight, and have to use starter fluid to get her fired up. I'm beginning to hate cold weather.

I slip and slide my way to the tire shop, realize I'm going to need a full face mask under the helmet if I don't want to freeze my nose off, and leave it to have studs put in the tires so I don't upend my bike and bust my ass on every corner.

Now it's time to see if my scumbag appearance fools anyone. The good news is my bruising and knots are gone, except for some puke-yellow tinges.

It's a little late for the lunch crowd, but the same bartender is working the bar who was there the last time I was in, with only three others bellied up...but one of them is Detective Tony DiAngelo, and he's drinking a cup of coffee at the bar, chatting with the other two guys.

He eyeballs me like I'd just crawled out of one of the dumpsters out back, but shows no signs of recognition and doesn't come down to throw me out of the joint. The bartender wipes the bar on the way down to where I've seated myself on a barstool, doesn't look happy, but asks, "What can I get you?"

"What's the…the soup today," I say, keeping my voice gravelly.

"Minestrone, as usual, and we got split pea."

"Coffee and split pea," I mumble, without any politeness.

"You got it," he says and moves away as if he wants no part of me.

Detective Tony downs his coffee and I can feel his eyes bore into me as he passes behind, and I exchange glances with him in the mirror behind the bar.

As I'm spooning in my soup, and fighting to chew some great French bread, I realize that my face is already getting a little tender from the two times I've bleached my beard out, but I'll soon solve that problem.

I return to the camper, with the Harley gripping the icy road enough to give me confidence about riding it, and feeling I'm home free with the disguise.

Bolting my armor back on my forearm over the cast, I wrap it in gauze so as to hide the spikes. I feel I'm getting closer to the point I'll get to try it out on some dope dealer's hard head or the across the soft flesh of his throat.

Chapter Ten

I dress layered up with Under Armor long johns, a sweat shirt, sweat pants, and my leathers. Pleased, I find a knit face mask in my gear. I push the sleeve of the Under Armor and sweatshirt up over my elbow—and luckily my leather jacket is loose enough to fit over the cast and iron work. Donning my helmet with its Plexiglas shield and some heavy duty riders gloves with gauntlets damn near to the elbow, I hope I'll stay warm as I set out on a mission of discovery. I picked up maps of the primary fields where Owens-McKittrick has rigs working—mostly Billings, Golden Valley, McKenzie, and Williams counties in North Dakota—and have what we think must be Speck's home and office located on a map.

There are RV's and campers and trailers everywhere as I head out 136th NW to the north of town, and I soon locate what turns out to be a double-wide a quarter mile east of the road, a luxury unit in both size and condition compared to most, where the GPS says Speck's Apple computer is to be found. There are a few lots with RV's and trailers a quarter mile north and east of Speck's place, but it's basically alone with nothing closer than a quarter mile. There are no outbuildings but the place is well maintained and the yard, the parking area, has been recently plowed. It's mid-afternoon and the trailer is surrounded by eight vehicles, most four-wheel drive late model pickup trucks. There's a service station and mini-market a quarter mile from his place back on the corner of 136th, so I return there, fill the Harley, get myself a cup of lousy coffee, and perch out near the country road to recon the mobile home for a while. No sign of life, but if it's full of boys who work most the night selling dope and women, who must be working girls, so it's likely they're still sacked out.

I decide to check out the oil fields and see if I can spot some Owens-McKittrick rigs and get a feel for things, and will swing back by the mobile home on my way in.

Even as warmly as I'm dressed, I soon decide the Harley is a lousy idea. I feel like my hands are frozen to the grips by the time I get a few miles out of town and turn toward one of the areas Owens-McKittrick works, and soon spot a rig painted red-lead bright orange. There're three guys working the service rig and a guy in a pickup watching, with the windows rolled up and him drinking from a chrome colored adult version of a sippy cup.

I idle up beside him and he rolls the window only half-way down. He's wearing a Owens-McKittrick emblem on his hard hat, and gray streaked red hair strings out from it. His beard, a week's worth, is red as well, but streaked with gray and his face is round and his nose and cheeks either show an alcoholic splotching or he's just come in out of the cold.

"What's up?" he asks.

"You hiring?"

"You worked a service rig before?"

"Nope, but I was a roustabout on a drilling rig down near Bakersfield for a couple of years, and in Wyoming before that." And was, before I went in the service.

He digs around and hands me a business card. "I don't hire. The office does. Go see them and unless you come up as a mass murderer you'll get hired."

"Thanks," I say. "How about if I am a mass murderer?"

He laughs, and grunts out, "So long as you didn't kill your co-workers or your boss you'll still get on."

I glance at the card, "You Ian McCuen?"

"Yeah."

I offer my hand. He looks a little put out, but rolls the window down the rest of the way and shakes with me.

"I owe you a tall cold one," I say, and settle back on the Harley.

"Make it a short strong one, and you're on."

"You got it." I use one of my aliases. "I'm Dick Strong."

He nods, and the window goes back up. I've worked around enough tool pushers to know they're best at sitting in the truck watching other guys work, and enjoying the fact they finally got off the drilling rig floor…or in this case, service rig.

The worst thing about using aliases is remembering who you were when you met someone. I carry four driver's licenses. My Nevada alias is Richard Head, since I have a twisted sense of humor…AKA Dick Head, a label assigned all of his jarheads by one of my long ago drill instructors. I also have business cards and a driver's license as Toby Ornot, Grubner Security, with a Salt Lake City address. I many times introduce my self as Toby Ornot to be. I smile as I change driver's licenses in my wallet. Another is John Mioff, my friends call me Jack, with a Ventura, California address. Peter Long is a Florida license as is Dick Strong, both of which are likely to cause comment when introduced to the ladies…but I play it straight, no pun intended. And my only legit license is Mike Reardon, Sheraton, Wyoming.

After I used Dick Strong, I remember that that's the name I gave Travis Speck when I talked to him at the bar. I'm going to have to change names if I've changed identities.

I check out another three fields until I'm damn near frozen to the marrow, then head back to the minimarket near Speck's trailer, at least the location of his computer, to warm my hands on lousy coffee and check out the double wide again.

I glance at my phone and see it's six p.m. by the time I get settled back on the Harley to watch the mobile home, and note that now there are only four vehicles parked in it's lot. I'm about ready to head back to the camper, pick up some clothes, and go to Anytime Fitness to shower and dress for a big night on the town, when a black crew cab pickup in the lot pulls from the parking lot to up near the door, and three girls run out and load up.

Firing up the Harley I head back to a parking place near the door of the minimarket and watch as the black Dodge heads our way, then dismount and head inside when the truck pulls into the lot and up to the gas pumps. I watch as a medium size muscle fuck who's driving gets out, hands one of the girls a credit card through the window and heads inside and she gets out. Under her overcoat which flares in the breeze, I can see she's dressed much as my new girlfriend Vanna was. She works the pump then jumps back inside while the truck fills up.

Oh, my buddy Pax is good. I have a picture of the guy who's pushing his way in the door in my file. He's one of the V guys Vanna mentioned, but his real name, at least the name he was booked under, is Vlad, not Victor or Vasily. He buys a twelve pack of cheap beer, starts out, then returns to the separate area of the store where the hard liquor is kept, asks the young lady behind the counter, and she fetches him a fifth of cheap whiskey. By the time he's back to the truck, he's popped the cap and taken a deep slug, and the girl has jumped back out into the cold and re-seated the nozzle. They fire it up, head out, and I follow.

The girl behind the counter calls after me as I push out the door, "No more coffee?"

But I wave over my shoulder and mount up, wait until they're a block down the road, and follow.

It's good and dark out when he drops the first pair of girls off downtown on one of the side streets, but a busy one with a line of cheesy bars, then heads four more blocks down the same drag and deposits the second pair.

I'd like to get back and get to the shower as I haven't enjoyed real hot water since leaving Vegas, but I'd also like to watch the girls, and maybe talk to one as soon as the other is picked up by a John. I'm sure I won't learn anything other than the price for a 'round the world' should I try and talk to them together. I back the Harley in between a couple of trucks and walk across the sidewalk and duck into the dark doorway of a building that's boarded up and looks to have recently had a fire…and stand and watch while the cold seeps into my bones.

I'm just about to head out and come back later, when a beat up Dodge truck slows, and the girls both flash their overcoats open and give the driver their most seductive looks and a glance at the goods. He speeds off, but in moments I can see he's circled the block. He stops, trades words with the girls, and the taller of the two climbs in and they're gone.

It's time to chit chat with another hooker.

Chapter Eleven

I park a half block away from where the girl has retreated into a doorway to get out of the wind, and wander down on foot.

She's lighting up a smoke as I near. Glancing up, she sees me coming and drops her hands, hiding the smoke behind her. I wonder if a hooker who smells like a Camel—that's the cigarette not the animal—has a little more trouble attracting a John than one who smells like Corral Number Five? Or I should say even Channel No. Five.

"Hey, darling, what's up?" I ask as she steps out of the doorway.

"Workin' hard for the money," she says, again attempting a seductive look. As she gets more into the light I can see she's Amer-Asian, or Euro-Asian, and pretty exotic looking for a working girl. She's got an accent, but I'm not good enough with the Asian ones to spot the origin.

"How much money you working hard for?" I ask, like I'm interested in plying her wears.

"You a cop?" she asks, only half getting serious.

I step back and spread my arms a little. "Do I look like the friggin' fuzz?"

"Got to ask. So, it's two hundred for the standard, a hun for a hummer, so long as I'm not away from my corner more than twenty minutes."

"Hells bells, girl, that's way better than Union contract."

"And I'm way better."

"What's your name, baby doll?"

"Well, it's not Baby Doll, it's Tiffany, cause I shine like a diamond."

"So, Tiffany, what's my price. Forget those other prices. I'm a working stiff."

"Why, honey, the last guy said my little sweet-thing was like a mare munching oats...he said I wasn't charging enough. I got her shaved so there be no bristle and the tight little thing is soft as a sow's ear. That last trick ask me to marry him three times in his twenty. So, like I said, it's two hundred for a standard, missionary style nothing kinky, or a single Ben Franklin for me to play you like a juice harp...so long as I'm not gone more than twenty minutes."

"You're daddy got you on a string, or what?"

"No, but he's got some serious hardware for any John keeps me beyond the time."

I laugh, then get serious and ask, "I don't imagine you've seen my ex-wife, Vanna, around?"

Her face falls and her tone goes nasty. "You are no John. Get the fuck away from me before I buzz my killer man up and he hardwares your dumb ass."

I shrug. "I was just wondering how my ex, Vanna, was getting along?"

"I do not know no shit about no other girls. Particularly no black bitch. Get away, you don't want your knees broke or your pencil dick shot off."

Again I shrug, then spin on my heel and head back for the Harley like I'm worrying about her pimp showing up to break my knees, fire it up and head to the camper to put this damn freezing-ass ride away, and head to the gym for a hot shower and a shave, if my face can take it. I've got a plant on goatee that I won't have to keep bleaching, and it's next in my bag of tricks.

It's plain that Vanna did work the street here, as I never mentioned she was black.

Although that last trick, looking for my ex-wife Vanna, worked about as well as an Obamacare website.

I go back to the camper and pick out some clothes to wear that will fit over my cast and armor, then head to Anytime Fitness for a short workout, a shower, a shave, and the application of my new decoration, a goatee.

The place is crowded, so I skip pushing weights as it's probably better if I rest the wrist anyway, but shower for thirty minutes on their gas bill and shave, trying to keep from engaging anyone in any kind of conversation, then return to the camper and spend an hour applying my new scraggly blond goatee and mustache. In addition to my custom sunglasses, I have a pair with non-prescription lenses, purely for disguise, and pull on a Carhartt stocking cap, with the stringy blond hair hanging out of the rear, sides and bangs, and am ready to give it the true test, Big Rosie's.

This time I drive the van, which no one should tie to me. I park in front and wander in, head hanging down, as mousy as a big guy can be. Buck Owens and the Buckaroos are knocking down *Tiger By The Tail* loud enough to drown out a passing freight train, and the place is, as usual, elbow to elbow. And I elbow my way to the bar and take up a position at the barmaid's station.

A tall Indian kid works the other end of the bar, a handsome kid...he could be Iron Eyes Cody's grandson.

The old redhead...Maggy as I recall...is working my end of the bar. If she doesn't make me, no one will. She gets within ten feet and stops short. I still haven't met her gaze, and still don't, but she comes on my way a little more slowly.

"What's it for you, bub?" she asks.

"Tall Greyhound, please," I mumble without looking up.

"Speak the fuck up," she commands.

"Tall Greyhound," I say louder, but still don't meet her eyes.

"You a local?" she asks.

"Omaha, Nebraska, come to get some work."

"Ain't ever'body," she says, and moves away to mix my drink. It's all I can do not to Cheshire grin, but that might give me up.

I throw a five on the bar and she returns with the drink, but just stands there. I give her my back and take a sip, then feel her whack me on the back. Still without looking up, I turn back and semi-face her.

"You must be a Nebraska corn-shucker, mother fucker. This is Bakken county. The drink is seven bucks. And speak the fuck up, I can't hear shit over that country crap."

I put two more on the bar, saying nothing, and she snatches them up. "Thanks, Midas. Don't bust your tight ass," she says with a growl and stomps away.

Again I want to smile, as I seem to be home free with the shaggy and stringy blond hair, and bad excuse for a goatee and stash.

Careful not to meet her gaze, I do carefully look over the crowd. In the very back corner, seventy five feet from me, I see three guys in a booth. One of them looks like the guy who came in the minimart and bought the bottle and twelve pack, the other is tall and thin, and the third guy is sitting on the outside of the booth with one of his massive cheeks hanging over the edge. If he doesn't go four hundred I don't know my heavyweights.

I start across to make a pass by them to make sure it's the boys Vanna was talking about, am elbowing my way through five couples on the dance floor—out of the hundred or more in the bar there's not more than ten women, including Maggy and two barmaids—and bump into a guy who's not dancing, but also working his way to the other side of the room.

"Watch it, asshole," he snaps, and I keep my eyes down.

"Sorry, man," I say.

"You fuckin' well should be."

I glance up enough to see the guy I seem to see everywhere, it's Tony DiAngelo, only this time in plainclothes...still, I bet he's working as he's dressed like he just climbed down from a steam tower or off an oil rig. I'm not surprised when he goes the same way I'm heading, and slips into a booth, one that will hold four but has the only two women in the place without men clinging to them, and with his back to the corner booth where the Ruskies are sipping and shooting the bull.

Since I've decided he's a good guy, and since it pays to have friends carrying shields, I decide to rat myself out and move straight to the booth and plop myself down across from him and next to an Indian girl who looks like she could kill and eat a grizzly for breakfast.

"Hey, man, I didn't mean to bump into you out there. Can I buy y'all a drink?"

Since I'm speaking in my normal voice, he eyes me carefully, then asks, accusingly, "I know you."

Chapter Twelve

DiAngelo's looking across the table like he'd like to pull on me.

"You do," I say. "But lets talk about it later?"

"You were in the club today, but I know you from the hospital."

"You do," I repeat. "But lets talk about it later."

He nods his head, looking a little confused. The girl on his right, across from me, is not half bad looking, and answers my question. "You can buy a drink, but it won't get you anywhere." So much for my natural charm.

"Speak for yourself, white eye," the big lady next to me says to her, laughs, and then gives me a grin showing a missing front tooth. She sighs a little too deeply. Pizza breath. Pizza with anchovies. Boy, I can pick 'em.

"We gotta go to the head," DiAngelo says, stands, and waves me up.

I rise, but hesitate long enough to tell the ladies, "I'll send one over. What are you drinking."

"A half-yard of Guinness," the big lady announces.

The other giggles and adds, "A grasshopper."

I nod and follow DiAngelo, who doesn't look particularly happy. I pause at the end of the bar away from where Maggy's working and tell the tall handsome Indian kid the girl's order and throw a twenty on the bar. "Keep the change," I say, getting a nod from the kid as I follow the detective into the hallway then into the restroom.

There's another guy in there taking a piss, and DiAngelo goes to the sink and washes his hands while the guy finishes and leaves without washing his.

DiAngelo gets about a foot away from me, eye to eye. "What the fuck are you doing? I'm on a stakeout here. I thought you were leaving town? What the fuck's with the blond—"

"Slow down, detective. Let's have breakfast or lunch tomorrow. You're onto the right guys, at least part of your problem. Go back to work and I'll find somewhere else to play. How about your daddy's joint at noon tomorrow?"

"Make it one fifteen. I don't like the lunch crowd, and breakfast is out. I'm working late."

"You're on. Good luck with the Russian boys."

He eyes me like I know too much, then nods his head and pushes his way out the door. I wait a good five minutes before I follow, then go out the back door, carefully checking to see there's not five guys waiting for me with pipes or baseball bats. I'm carrying my coat thinking I'll pull it on while heading for my van, then am glad it's in hand as my armor and its spikes are only covered by a couple of wrappings of gauze.

There's not five guys, but there's one guy, a very big guy, standing having a smoke near a garbage dumpster and just beyond it is a snow bank where the plow has stacked it six feet high.

And it's one of my Indian buddies. Big John Broken Toes if my memory serves, three hundred twenty pounds the last time he was arrested; easy to tell the difference as this one has braided hair to the center of his back. The other guy, Many Horses, is taller and a measly two eighty, and keeps his mop in an Elvis doo lap. Big John glances at me then turns, quartering away.

I've promised myself not to test the condition of my wrist for a while, but this is just too good not to take advantage of.

He starts to cough and turns his back completely to me.

I guess it's time to test the wrist. I drop the coat and in three strides whack him a solid one across the very crown of his head with the bottom bar on the wrist armor. It's a blow that should have dropped him like the bag of shit he is, but he merely oofs and sags a little before he regains his feet...so I spin and side kick him behind his knee, and that folds him. He goes to his knees then pitches forward on his face. With everything I have, like I'm going for a fifty year field goal, I kick him in the ribs and he oofs again...the hell of it is I lose my footing on the back stroke on the damn icy pavement and my feet go out from under me.

He's up on all fours, crabbing forward, and I lunge after him. He's trying to turn to face me, and this time I give him a forearm and drag it across his face, the spikes do their work and he's spouting blood from his forehead. I again get my footing as he rolls and sits on his massive butt, trying to wipe the blood out of his eyes.

Scrambling up, I step back and wind up. This time the kick catches him on the point of his chin, and his eyes roll up in his head and he goes to his back, his head at the base of the snow bank.

He's out cold. I'm tempted to drag some snow on top of him and hope no one finds him until spring, but I've yet to know enough to sentence him, not even to frost bite and the loss of his ugly nose and Dumbo ears.

I give him a couple more kicks in the ribs, just for good measure, hoping I've broken at least three or four, then gather up my coat and haul ass to the van before someone else wanders out for a smoke.

Since I don't want the prick to freeze to death, at least until I know that he deserves an icy grave, I call Rosie's on one of my throw away phones and tell them there's some drunk about to buy the farm in a snow-bank outside their back door.

"Who is this?" the girl who answers asks.

"Jack Frost," I say, and disconnect.

I'm feeling a lot better. There's nothing quite like the spice of revenge to flavor up your night.

Turning on the Sirius, I find some Credence Clearwater and smile all the way back to the camper. I kicked ass and didn't even split a knuckle. I have to buy my new sculptor a tall cold one if I run into him in a pub.

And to put a cherry on top, my camper water's thawed and working.

So I add some ice cold tap water to a couple of shots of Jack Daniels and a couple of ice cubes, find a good Louis L'Amour novel I've been wanting to read, and curl up. It's midnight, and I've got to get used to staying up extra late as dope dealers don't go to work early, so I plan to read a couple of hours.

Tomorrow I try to make a friend and compatriot out of the Italian stallion, Detective Tony DiAngelo, even if he does use the beauty shop to do his full perfectly-coifed head of hair.

Chapter Thirteen

Late is never in my bag of tricks unless I have a tactical reason to be so, so I arrive at DiAngelo's after a lazy morning with L'Amour's *The Sacketts*, cold cereal, hot coffee—thanks to my water thawing—and a spit bath will real hot water. I have a shower in the camper, but have yet to give it a try as it sprays the whole tiny bathroom and besides, I'm shoulder to shoulder with the walls and have to duck my head. A shower in the camper might result in a crick in my neck.

It's one forty when DiAngelo finally wanders in, walks right past me to the kitchen door, then an older guy who I presume is his father comes out of the kitchen and they b.s. for another

fifteen minutes before he disdains to join me in a corner table near the front, but it's out of the view of passersby through the windows. I don't want it thought that I'm friendly with the law, in fact, just the opposite, so I'm not excited about being seen with the fuzz.

He sits, orders some dish that's not on the menu, and I tell the girl, "two," presuming that he's well versed on what's really good that comes out of a kitchen which is, at the moment, smelling like the best of the south of Italy.

It's soup, served with a half a loaf of great hard-crusted bread.

"So," I ask, "what are we eating?"

"Zuppa trippa."

"Soup, okay, what kind of soup?"

He laughs as if I'm going to run for cover when he tells me.

"Tripe, the lining of a cow's gut."

"Wow, it's good. I've had lots of menudo, the Mexican version, but this is every bit as good."

"If my old man comes out of the kitchen you better say it's the best thing you've ever eaten."

"Damn near is."

He looks at me with new respect, then asks, "So, how the hell did you know about those boys being Russian?"

"I haven't exactly leveled with you, detective. I'm on a private contract here to see who's screwing up a company's formerly great safety record."

"Insurance investigator?" he asks. Then, before I can answer, suggests, "I don't drink on duty unless I'm undercover, but you should have a glass of red with that."

I nod my head and he yells at the bartender in Italian, and he delivers a glass filled to the very brim with something that looks like it will put permanent purple stains on my teeth, but on first sip tastes like Ambrosia.

"So," he continues, "insurance investigator?"

"No, sir. Private security. I carry a bail enforcement officers badge, but do little of it."

"So, who's your employer?"

"Can't say."

His eyes narrow. "What the fuck do you mean, you can't say?"

"I'm contractually obligated not to divulge my employer."

"You met Amber at Owens-McKittrick, so you must be working for them?"

"Can't say, but that could have just been part of my investigation. I'll try and meet with all the oil well service companies before I'm through...here and on the Montana side."

He seems to chew on that a moment, then shrugs his shoulders. "So, what do you know about the Russians and human trafficking?"

"To be truthful, I'm more interested in kicking the stilts out from under the dope dealers—"

"Same guys," he says.

"So, we have the same target if for different reasons."

"Yeah, but all it takes to get a bail enforcement shield is two hundred pounds of stupidity and about forty bucks for the brass...you have no authority in North Dakota, or in neighboring Montana, or hell, anywhere so far as I know so why are we having this meeting unless you're planning on being a CI?"

"Mutual interest. And I have plenty of authority if I have a contract from a bondsman...you should catch up on your Supreme Court rulings." I know that by CI he means confidential informant. I add, just so he knows I do my homework, "In North Dakota, the surety, the bondsman, may arrest a defendant at any place or may empower any person of suitable age and discretion to do so...and I think that's a verbatim quote of the law. I'm 'any person of suitable age' in case you haven't noticed.

And, by the way, I carry the proper concealed carry authority."

He laughs. "I already made the lump in the center of your back. You weren't getting out of here without me calling you on it. Still, no matter, I can't divulge anything to you as you have no standing in law enforcement."

I smile and shrug. "Then I'm not obligated to you in any way to divulge what I know, and unless you have the best computer crew in the country, like I have, and warrants to snoop like you're the NSA, I know one hell of a lot more than you do."

"How about I drag your ass in and hold you for a while since I think you're withholding evidence? And maybe for suspicion of assault and battery...it seems some old boy got the double dog shit kicked out of him right about the time you walked out the back door of Rosie's."

"To be somewhat less than polite, detective...go fuck yourself. If you're trying to assure you don't learn anything from me, ever, haul me in on some bullshit charge. It'll only enhance my standing among the shitheads I'm trying to get next to." Then I hold up my arm with the cast under my coat. "Besides, I've got a broke wing...wouldn't do to be scraping."

Again, he laughs, only louder. Then he sighs deeply. "Okay, I'll show you mine after you show me yours. What do you have?"

"First, give Detective Andre Bolenger with Vegas PD a call. He'll clue you in on me." Bolenger and I bounced off each other several times during the last gig I had in Vegas, circling each other like two old hound dogs, but ended up being friends, and with mutual respect. "Second, I'll have to find a copy machine but in the meantime, give me an email address and I'll have some stuff sent to you. Cell phone number too, if you would. We'll talk again."

He nods, makes a note on another napkin and hands it over, then his attention is distracted. I'm rising, and turning when I see it's the beautiful copper-blond Amber entering. She moves our way, and I drop my gaze and brush by her. I get no sign of recognition, and hear her ask, "Hey, Tony. I was down the street and thought I might catch you here. Who was that?"

As I push through the door, I have to smile as I hear, "Some bum. I ran him out of here."

"Oh."

So, I have a good contact with local law enforcement—I'll pray he's not a crooked cop—so now it's time to get serious.

Chapter Fourteen

I hit the gym again to work up a sweat, shower, but don't shave as I want the phony goatee surrounded by stubble, and dress again in my dumpster diver dregs. I've got to watch it as it grows in darker than my bleached brows, wig, and phony goatee, so I'll have to shave it every three days or so or risk getting a raw face from bleaching my cheeks and neck as well.

I've got a personal hotspot on my iPhone which provides Wi-Fi for my computer, so I return to the camper and email Pax for some help. My email is routed thru a friend in Mumbai, India, then his brother in Malta, and is very hard to track, thanks to the machinations of Weatherwax Internet Service. I ask him to track Speck's iPhone as I'd like to dog his trail for a while. I know where his Apple laptop lives, in the double wide out off 136th, and now it's time to discover where he travels and who else he runs with.

Pax has discovered there's a Cadillac registered to Speck down in El Paso, and sends me his license plate number, the color of the car—candy apple red—and an address where the iPhone is at the moment. He even emails me a .jpg showing Google Earth's areal picture of the building. A run down barn on a farm northeast of town, away any oil fields. It's a twenty minute drive to locate the place, but I do and it's truly remote, sheltered by the hills from view from the small county road. It snowed a couple of inches last night, and there are no vehicle tracks going into the place, and the gate is locked...but it's a cheap master lock and I pick it in three heartbeats and only drive far enough so I can see into the wide and deep coulee where the barn's located. There is smoke snaking up from a pipe on the roof, and a couple of pickups, one black, one canary yellow—no Cadillac—are parked near the double barn doors. Another road leads toward the back of the property. If Speck was here he's gone now, or he's driving a pickup, or with someone who is. Or his phone is there and he's not, which is unlikely.

A hundred yards from the barn squats the remnants of a farmhouse, brick chimney and a pile of rubble, which says to me that the farmhouse burned some time ago. There's also a windmill, but it's broken down and not turning. I back the van away, walk the few yards back to the crest of the hill and study the place for a few minutes through my binocs. It would be a little hard to explain the picked lock if someone wandered in behind me, so I beat a trail, locking the gate behind me, concerned that I've left tracks in the snow.

It's time I checked in with the colonel, so I give him a call.

"Where the hell you been?" he answers, and I presume I'm the only one who has a number to this particular phone.

"Been busy. Somewhere we can meet?"

"Hell, I've snuck by your camper and truck a half dozen times. I was afraid one of these assholes got lucky and buried you out in the boondocks. I've been worried as hell—"

"Out of town a while. Sorry, colonel—"

"It's Oscar, remember."

"Yes, sir. Somewhere we can parlay for a half hour?"

"I'm heading home in a half hour." He gives me his address. "There's a city park a block from my place. Drive by the front, count the houses to the corner next to the park. Leave your van there and hoof it down the alley and come in through the back gate. I'll have a shot of Jack waiting to warm you up."

"Yes, sir. How many houses are you from the corner."

"Hell, I don't know...six or seven."

"Okay. See you in an hour or so."

It's just getting good and dark when I arrive at his back gate, which he's left ajar. Nice house, maybe the nicest on the block. A lady, I presume his wife, is working at the sink when I reach the back door, and start to knock, then reel back when a Rott hits the back door hard enough, and loud enough, that I think he's coming through. I damn near fall off the back porch.

In seconds the lady is at the door, yelling at the dog. "Brutus, down. Down!" She opens the door and I can hear the low rumble of his growl...sounds like an idling Mack truck.

"I'm sorry. Big O is showering and was supposed to have Brutus back there with him. You must be Mike. Come on in." She notes my hesitancy, and laughs. "He's fine. He'd eat you if I wasn't here, but now he'll lick you to death."

"Yes, ma'am," I say and walk on in where angels might fear to tread.

"Brutus, this is Mike. He's an old buddy of papa's."

The low rumble stops and he walks right up and puts his muzzle in my crotch, and for a second I fear I'm a half second from never having a reason to have an assignation again. Then I step back and offer a hand and he gives it a good sniff, then as promised, a lick. I scratch his ears, and then he wanders away into a family room and curls up in front of the roaring fire in a firebox big enough contain a decent sized hog to roast for the next luau.

I watch him, then turn back to the lady. "Yes, ma'am, Mike Reardon." I extend my hand and instead of taking it, she sticks a glass of booze into it.

"I'm Houston, the first mate around here."

I have to smile. "I've heard the colonel called a lot of things, some of them not so polite, but Big O...that's a new one."

"A hell of a compliment coming from a guy's wife, particularly one fifty three years old, wouldn't you say?"

"Yes, ma'am, I would, but who are you talking about, as you're sure as hell's hot not over thirty three years old. I figured you for the trophy wife or girlfriend more like thirty three."

"Aren't you a smooth talking devil?"

"Hey, jarhead," the colonel calls from exiting the hall into the family room, "watch your step. I can still take you." The big Rott, Brutus, trots over and nuzzles up to him to get his ears scratched again.

"No doubt, colonel...not fair through, you've got half a Roman legion helping you."

He corrects me again. "Oscar." Then asks, "She make you a decent drink?"

"Yes, sir."

"Come on back to my study and let mama fix some chow."

I smile all the way to the hall. I haven't had a real home cooked meal in a month of Sundays, and I presume I'm invited.

"It's meatloaf and mashed, nothing fancy," she calls after me.

"Fabulous," I say over my shoulder.

"Isn't that same as bullshit in Marine-lingo?"

I wave over my shoulder and hustle after the colonel, who still walks like a freight train rolls.

He sits behind a big rosewood desk. The walls are covered with memorabilia of the Corps, and framed medals are everywhere as well as dozens of pictures of him in exotic places, and a few of him with prominent politicians.

"Quite a room," I offer.

"Bullshit. All that matter's is today. How are you doing out there in the world of dope dealers and pimps?"

I spend fifteen minutes and down my whole drink while filing him in or what's happened.

"I heard about the broken wrist," he says. "Sorry about that."

"Shit happens," I say, and pull up my sleeve and show him my armor plating. "Mama told me to make lemonade when life hands you lemons. I already proved it's usefulness on the big Indian I mentioned."

"You remember the rules?"

I laugh. "Yeah, most of them."

"Just in case…have a plan, have a second plan as the first one will probably go to hell; always cheat, always win…the only unfair fight is one you lose; in ten years no one will remember the tactics, the details, the weaponry…they'll only remember who won or who lost; be polite, and have a plan to kill everyone you come across; and last, have the biggest weapon and even if you don't…use the one you have first and fastest."

I nod, and laugh again. I heard it from him at least a hundred times in Iraq.

"Let's eat. I've got some paperwork for you. Don't get out of here without it."

"Yes, sir."

"Fuck that yes sir, I had enough of that in the Corps."

"Semper fi," I say, and laugh again.

Chapter Fifteen

When I get back to the camper, there's a party going on in the converted school bus; the trailer and the other Lance camper is dark. I can smell the weed as soon as I step out of my van. Two guys stand outside the bus, both dressed like they came directly from the rig.

There's a big, dark colored, Ford Expedition parked between my rigs and the bus, and another crew cab pickup, also dark colored, on the other side. New vehicles to the gathering of RV's.

As I head for the camper, all sounds eclipsed by the heavy metal music thumping from inside the blacked out windows, one of them yells at me. "Hey, man, we're out of mix. You got any Cokes or shit like that?"

I just happen to have a six pack under my sink, and yell back, "Hold on." It's time I meet my neighbors, if for no other reason to ascertain if they're only recreational users, or part of the real problem.

I return and hand over the six pack, and stick out a hand. "Toby," I say. I realize that both guys are Hispanic when I get closer.

The shorter one, with a pot belly and weird green eyes, offers a hand, "Hey, man. You okay. I'm Al." I shake, and turn to the other, who's taller, and way, way thinner, sallow and sour faced with sunken cheeks. Cheeks that sport a couple of tear drop tats under one eye. And he's wearing a pinky ring that looks to be over a caret, if it's real.

"They call me Tamale," he says, without a smile and with a single, clammy, pump of the handshake.

"Okay, guys. Nice to meet the neighbors. Smells like good weed. You got any I can buy."

The short one is doing the talking for both. "We ain't your neighbors, man, we just partying with Curly."

"Curly?" I ask, not pressing the offer to buy.

"Yeah, Curly's bus. We just dropped buy." He walks back to the two-stair entrance to the bus and bangs on the door. He's got to bang hard, as even face to face we're having to yell over the Black Sabbath that's rocking the world. He bangs harder, and the folding doors part.

"Come out and meet the neighbors," Al yells over the racket.

"Asshole complaining about the noise?" the guy, whose hair hangs to his waist, asks, and eyes me with disdain. He's got tats up his neck all the way to the jawline.

"No, man, he brought us some mix, lighten the fuck up."

He nods demurely at Al, and it's obvious who's the alpha male in this crowd, at least so far. Then he adds, "too fucking cold outside. Come on in."

The long hair waves me over, and I follow the two Hispanics up and into the bus. I don't have to buy any grass to get high, all I have to do is breath.

The place is pretty well tricked out, with, of course, all the seats removed and replaced by cheap upholstered pieces and a couple of beat up coffee tables. The back is partitioned off into what I'd imagine is a bedroom and maybe even a toilet and shower—if so it doesn't get used much, as the one who I presume is Curly, who's dirty blond hair is long and straight, looks as if he hasn't had it in the shampoo for a month or more. Along the partition wall on this side is a short counter, with sink and refrigerator. A cabinet is overhead.

And the boys aren't the only partygoers. Three girls are flopped on the upholstered pieces; there are enough tats in the bus that a one-color prison artist must have been kept busy for most of his term, plus some store-bought ones adorning the girls.

"That's Curly," Al says, as the long hair returns to a spot in the middle of the three, all of whom would be decent looking if they didn't appear to have been pulled through a wringer backwards. None of the three could be over twenty five, but all have had some serious miles on their odometers.

Curly sort of waves over his shoulder as he flops down.

"Hey, man," Al says, "show some hospitality. Get the *pendajo* a joint or drink or some fucking thing. He did us a solid."

Curly pokes one of the girls with an elbow, "Do what Big Al says." And she jumps up, and moves over to where I'm still standing, having to bend my neck a little as even dead center in the bus the clearance is not quite adequate.

She eyes me up and down, through bloodshot watery peeps, like I'm a popsicle, even though I'm in dumpster diver regalia, and mumbles, "Hey, Mondo man, you want a bomber? I just rolled a fat one." I have to smile as I notice that each of her nails, both fingers and toes, is painted a different color. She adds, "I'm Betty Boop, that there is Angela, and the dip shit in the glasses is Zelda."

But I don't laugh at the nails, only shrug, nod at the other girls, and offer, "Don't smoke. You got a beer?"

"The man is righteous," she says. Then adds, "And probably a real fuckin' bore."

"You a fucking cop?" Curly addresses me for the first time, and his tone is not friendly.

I reach over and take a joint out of the fingers of the nearest skank and take a deep draw and hand it back. "Do I look like a pig to you," I snarl at him, and they all laugh. "Did you notice the Nevada plates on my rigs?"

It's Curly's turn to shrug.

The one with the bloodshot eyes walks to the back and fishes a beer out of the little fridge and returns and hands it to me.

I note that Tamale has an eagle, globe and anchor tat on the back of his hand, so I ask, "Where'd you serve?"

He eyes me and growls, "Did three in Huntsville and a couple in road camps in Louisiana."

I can't help but smile, as I meant in the service, but just nod.

We hang out. I'm into my third beer, the girls into about their fifth rum and coke, and I'm half high from just breathing the atmosphere, when I finally dig my phone out and, acting as if I'm checking my email, manage to get pictures of all of them. Finally I stand, stretch, and yawn. "Hey, thanks for the good neighbor stuff. If there's anything I can do for y'all, just bang on the camper door," I head for the stairs. So-called Big Al, who's not really so big, is in the last chair near the door, and I stop. He's a little bleary eyed, and talking with a bit of a slur, so I figure it's a good time to ask again, "Hey, Al...or is it Alfredo or?"

"I ain't no fuckin' wop, it's Alverado, but nobody...nobody calls me that but...but my mamacita."

"Okay, Big Al. You got some weed I can buy?"

"I got two fuckin' tons, my man. You want to deal...to hustle some real scratch...or just...or just fuck around?"

"I could probably deal a few o's."

"Not tonight, Toby. I got to check you out. What's your last name?"

"Ornot."

"Or yes, or no, or not," he manages with a slur and a laugh. "Okay. Maybe I come by tomorrow...maybe not, Ornot," he laughs like he's made the joke of the year.

"Cool," I say, and check out.

Making a quick round of the parking lot, I note the license numbers and make and model of the Bus, the Expedition, and the GMC crew cab pickup before I climb into the camper.

I send the pics and all the info I have to Pax before I grab *The Sacketts* for a chapter or two.

I hate having some scumbags like my neighbors knowing where I sack out, but that's the way it is, at least for a while. You got to pay to play. I hit the sack, check the time and see it's midnight, so I set the alarm for three AM.

I got a little more biz before I'm through messing with my neighbors.

Chapter Sixteen

This tech age of ours is pretty amazing. I can now buy a GPS tracker for twenty five bucks including the shipping, so I have a half-dozen in my bag of tricks.

At three AM the alarm goes off and I'm up and out—I should have done more than just pull on my Carhartt pants, coat, and phony Uggs. I listened for but did not hear any heavy metal music blasting from the bus when I awoke, so I'm sure my neighbors have either passed out, or left, and if the vehicles are gone I'm on a fool's mission.

But they still rest, now covered with a dusting of snow. Seeing the bus looks dark and quiet as a tomb, I get about ten steps out of the camper before I'm real sorry I didn't pull on my long johns, but charge forward.

The tracker is small enough it fits in a magnetic key-keeper, so one goes under the back bumper of the Expedition and one under that of the GMC, and I hustle back to the camper, and find I've left the damn door ajar and it's down to about ten degrees inside. But I have one more chore. I email Pax with the code numbers for the trackers, and only then hit the sack again. I chatter until the sheets warm up, and then have no trouble getting back to sleep.

I'm normally an early riser, but sleep in, dozing actually, until I hear the doors working on the bus. And, as I suspected, it's the one who call's himself Al who slogs through the snow to the Expedition, with two of the three girls behind. The extra-ugly one who said he's called Tamale is close behind, but moves to the GMC and fires up and is gone. I hear the Ford grind away and finally fire up, and he, too, drives away. I guess Zelda with the glasses and Curly are a pair.

This little town must be dope dealer heaven as I was in town an hour before I got offered meth or coke, and my neighbors have a visitor who claims to have two tons of weed. One never knows, it might actually be only two ounces, but he's driving a nice rig and was wearing a pinky ring that looked to be a caret, if it's not a zircon.

As Vegas is Pacific time and North Dakota mountain time, I'm an hour ahead of Pax, so I head for Gramma Sharon's, which is reputed to have the best breakfast in town. And it must be okay, as even at nine fifteen I have to wait for a spot. I pick up a copy of the Williston Herald on the way in, and get halfway through the front page before the waitress gets to me. I finish the above the fold stories, including one about a young lady, nicely worded to only infer she was a lady of the night, being murdered in a downtown alley. I'm halfway through my sausage and eggs when I feel my phone vibrate, and fish it out to discover I don't have to phone Pax as he's calling me.

"Hoora," I answer.

"My man, you have stumbled into a den of vipers," he says, then chuckles.

"Snake killin' is what I'm paid for. Specifics, please?"

"The only one of the girls who I got anything on is the one you said was named Zelda. She's been arrested there locally for prostitution and had some grass, but less than an ounce. She was out in a day on her own recognizance. Nothing on the other two, at least not yet. Zelda's an alias, by the way, real name is Martha Gatsby...which I presume has somehow gained her the nickname of one the Fitzgerald characters in *The Great Gatsby*."

"Yeah, yeah," I offer with some sarcasm, "you're literate."

"Fuck you, Farley."

"So, the boys. What's with the boys, "Curly, Larry and Moe?"

"The California license plate was a dead giveaway for Curly. AKA Charles or Charley Hotchkiss, from Oakland. Released from Corcoran State a year ago after doing a nickel for sale of a controlled substance...and the super-duper ugly one, Tamale, he's from El Paso, probably illegal, if he's the only guy I found with the nickname Tamale who looked like this butt-fuck. If you had some more on his tats I might do better. If he's this Tamale he did a spell in Huntsville for dealing. And he has a dishonorable from the Corps for dealing while at Pendleton. Real name Guillermo Soto, if that's him. And the prize is Alverado Cenzano, street name Two Cents, cause the scoop is he once killed a guy on a bet for two cents. He escaped from Atascadero State Hospital...that's a great place if your criminally insane...four years ago. They'd really like to have him back, but since there was no bondsman, there's no bond, and no bond, no bounty. He was a bad, bad boy and killed and raped a half dozen women, including one in her seventies who was a matron at some homeless shelter he was using. He's a scum-suckin' amoral pig. Take his ass down, hard, if you get the chance."

"My pleasure. If that's it, give me location on sweet Al's Expedition and I'll wander over and see what he's up to. I ask if I could buy a few bags from him for resale, and he's, and I quote, checking out Toby Ornot...so put some bad shit up on the web about old Toby."

"My pleasure," he parrots me. "Looks like Cenzano is half way across town, heading east on 11th...oops, he turned. Hold on...he pulled up and stopped."

I go back to my sausage and eggs for a bite, then he adds, all I get is a couple of private residences

"Cool, thanks. Check you later."

Three more fast bites and I'm done. I head out to see if I can spot his car, and am going down 11th when I notice a candy apple red Cadillac coming my way. I don't really get a good look at the driver as a furniture van blocks my view about the time he passes, but how many candy apple Cad's can there be in Williston. I let him get a block by and flip a U-turn and follow for several blocks.

The Mercy Medical Center. He pulls in there and parks close to the emergency room. Then ambles in. It's no emergency as far as he's concerned if his casual walk is an indicator.

I park a couple of lanes away, and follow, but rather than the emergency room door, I head for the Caddy and slip another GPS device in a key keeper under the back bumper, and only then head for the main entrance, enter, and ask the candy striper the way to emergency. She's a cute little thing, if that can be said of a blue-hair.

She has a great smile. "You can go back outside, or head over there and pick up the red line and it will lead right there."

So I do. And the red line leads me via a couple of turns in a hallway wide enough for two gurneys to pass, to a pair interior swinging doors leading into the emergency room. There's a small glass panel in each door, so I pause and check things out, and it's a good thing I do as I see Speck talking to a nurse who's seated behind a desk.

She looks very serious, and he nods a couple of times then heads for the outside door, presses through, and is gone.

So I decide to see what I can wheedle out of the nurse, and push through. Out of a door leading off the hall, before I'm halfway to the desk nurse, comes a flash from my recent past. A sandy haired blue eyed beauty who nursed me during my stay.

"Inga," I say, and she looks up from the chart she's reading while walking.

Chapter Seventeen

"Why, if it isn't a former patient of the trouble maker variety," Inga says, but she's smiling.

"Dick Strong," I say, and then have to think if that's the name I used.

"I think I prefer Richard," she says, and smiles and shakes her head.

"Okay, if you're calling I'll answer to anything."

She gets serious. "You're back. Your wrist giving you trouble?"

I'm not real excited about her seeing my armor, and as she reaches for the arm I fold it behind my back.

"Heck no, you were my nurse. It's perfect."

"So you just like the smell of an emergency room."

It's my turn to laugh, then I add, "No, ma'am, but you might help me."

"How's that?"

Let me count the ways, I think, but don't say, but rather point to the desk where Speck talked to the nurse, and wave Inga behind me, and she follows.

A pudgy little freckled blond, glances up. "Hi, young lady. You were just talking to a thin faced guy with a scar—"

"I was," she says, glancing up, then at Inga, who nods.

"Can you tell me what he's asking about?"

She looks doubtful, then turns to Inga. "Miss Johannson?"

I'm fishing my wallet out as they exchange doubtful looks, and flash the brass. Sometimes the bail enforcement badge works, sometime not. Depends upon how close they look, and what they know about the law.

"Go ahead," Inga says to her.

"He was asking about a young lady who expired here last night. I guess he hadn't seen the paper and didn't know she didn't make it."

I did see the paper. "May I see the body?"

Again she looks at Inga, who shrugs.

The nurse offers, "A diener wheeled her out just as I showed up at work at seven."

"So, where?" I ask, having been around morgues enough to know that a diener is an assistant in that facility.

"She'd be in the basement, the door says autopsy, but it's also the morgue."

I turn to Inga. "How about showing me the way."

She smiles, but shakes her head no. "I'll get a candy striper."

"I'd rather it be you."

"I'll walk you back to the waiting room and the lady at the desk will page one for you."

"You're a hard case, Miss Johannson. I noticed the girl did say miss, not missus."

"How do you know we don't all go by miss in the hospital?" Her smile is devastating.

"So, miss, how would you like to have dinner with me."

She laughs again, and we arrive at the waiting room, and I'm properly ignored as she asks the lady at the desk to page someone, waves over her shoulder, and strides away.

A skinny young girl who looks as if she can't be over seventeen leads me down, then stops nervously ten feet from the door. "You don't mind showing yourself in," she says.

"Not your favorite place?" I ask.

And she shakes her head so hard I think she might dislocate a disk.

I wave, "thanks," and push my way inside a small waiting room without a reception desk, and only six chairs, so I push my way into another room, which is all stainless steel except for the dropped ceiling and it's some expanded metal, surrounding lots of florescent lights.

Two stainless tables are centered in the room, the far wall is lined with a half dozen doors obviously with drawers and rolling shelves for bodies.

I'm not surprised to see a draped body on one table, a man with a white apron covering most of him, and another in suit and tie.

"Why am I not surprised?" the suit asks as he eyes me.

"Dang," I say, "if it's not my favorite detective."

"Yeah," Tony DiAngelo says, "yours and half the worlds. Did you know the deceased and are here for an I.D., otherwise, as usual, you're where you shouldn't be."

"Let me take a look and I'll let you know if I know her."

He waves me over, and introduces me to the doc as I come. "This is Doc Thompson."

I nod, but don't offer my hand as he has a scalpel in one and the other looks a little sticky, besides, he has on rubber gloves.

He doesn't seem to mind and instead of shaking, reaches up and pulls the sheet down a modest distance.

"Jesus," I manage. Of course her skull cap is loose as he's removed the brain, but even as horrendous as that is, the condition her face is worse. She's been beaten far beyond someone doing so for a robbery. This is a beating of either pure rage, or to make a point with the living.

"I do think I know her, but it's hard to tell. And I never did get her name. If she's who I think she is she was working a street corner and was a surprisingly good looking girl, Eurasian, I'd guess, but don't know." A good looking girl...or she was."

"I've got some mug shots on her, and you're right. What did she charge you?" DiAngelo asks, and seems serious.

"I haven't paid for a piece since the last time I was in London ten years ago, and got the crabs from that mistake. No, I was just looking for a little info."

"More info than I needed. Let's get out of here. Let's go to the cafeteria and get some coffee."

We do.

After we fill a couple of coffee cups and get a seat, he chides me, "I keep looking in my in box, in my email, and on my carrier pigeon for that 'show me yours' you were gonna send."

"I haven't found a copy machine yet."

"Right. Drop by the department and I'll have it copied for you."

"Don't think I ought to be spending a lot of time eating donuts with you boys, not if I want to get next to the bad boys of North Dakota."

"So, are you?"

"Not doing bad. Partied it up with a few last night, followed one here—"

"Who?" He asks, suddenly interested.

"Speck's his name. Drives a candy apple caddy."

He nods knowingly. "He's upper mid-level, probably was checking on his girl."

"You think he did her?" I ask.

"Kill the goose that laid the golden egg...I doubt it. Not unless she went way off the reservation."

We talk for the better part of an hour, some of it getting to know each other. Other than the fact he was an Air Force dick, he's a good guy. More and more I think I can level with him, so I decide to actually send him most of what I know so far...besides, it's the only way I'm going to get anything out of him. Show me yours.... I hold back the location of the barn and burned out farmhouse where I saw the girls, and will continue to hold back on locations where I might be involved in activities law enforcement might not endorse.

Chapter Eighteen

After DiAngelo leaves the cafeteria I text Pax and give him DiAngelo's cell phone number and email address and ask him to email him almost all the info I've collected, including the pics. Now we'll see if he shows me his. I also give him the code number on the GPS device I've put on Speck's Cad.

By the time I reach my van, my phone vibrates and it's a text from Pax telling me some GPS coordinates and that Speck has driven over thirty miles to the northwest, and as I have nothing else on my plate, I decide to wander out into the oil fields and see what he's up to.

On the way out I pass what seems to be a daily event in the Bakken, a mud tanker truck has jackknifed and slid off the road into the ditch, turning over. It reminds me of a turtle on it's back, unable to right itself. There's already a half dozen pickup trucks parked nearby, so I idle past and pick up my speed to a dangerous thirty miles an hour on the ice. It happens so often the wrecks have their own Facebook page, *Fail of the Day*, one of the fastest growing pages on Facebook. I guess the whole world loves a good fuck-up.

Finding the GPS quadrant that Pax has sent me, where Speck's car remained for a half hour before he's headed back to town, as Pax has reported in another text, I'm not surprised to see it's one of Owens-McKittrick's crew camps. A dozen and a half doublewide trailers, each capable of housing a dozen cribs and a bathroom and shower room, are placed around a company store and café, of sorts. Between each of the trailers is enough room to park a dozen trucks.

It's an off time and there are only a couple of trucks parked near the café so I pull up and wander in to check the place out. It's fat dumb and happy time.

A burly old boy with salt and pepper chin whiskers is behind the counter, sipping a cup of coffee, and waiting for another shift change which I'm sure will fill the joint. There's only one other customer in the place, and he's in a far corner in front of one of those electric fireplaces, also sipping coffee, and coughing his head off between sips.

I go to the counter and order my own cup.

"How's business?" I ask.

"Captured audience," he says. "Wish I owned the place."

He pours me a cup in a thick sided crockery mug, and asks, "Cream or sugar?"

"Nope, but a little help maybe. I'm supposed to meet a guy here, driving a candy apple Cadillac. Seen him around?"

"Yeah, left here about a half hour ago."

"Damn, I was supposed to meet him and another guy—"

"Nickleston, he's the superintendent of this field. He left too…probably back to town to his office. Dumb fucks sat out in Nickleston's truck in the cold and jawed for fifteen minutes. They musta burned up a gallon of gas so they could run the heater."

"Yeah, that's him. Good coffee by the way."

"Thanks."

"So Nickleston and the guy in the Cadillac already met without me?"

"That's it, partner. Looks like you missed out."

"What's the guy's name...the Cadillac guy?"

"I thought you were supposed to meet him...and you don't know his name?" He's getting suspicious.

"Yeah, I met him in the bar last night, and, I'm embarrassed to say, forgot his name. And he said he had a job for me if I'd meet him here."

"Johnson is all I know. I think Nickleston called him Jack."

So Speck is using an alias too. Why am I not surprised. I flip a five on the bar and say thanks, and head for the door.

"Man, you ain't too hungry for a job, you can tip three bucks for a lousy cup of coffee."

I stop and turn back, "If you're complaining I'll take my change." He has no way of knowing I'm actually tipping for the info.

He laughs. "No complaint from me, partner."

"By the way," I ask, "where's Nickleston's office."

"BP owns the field. And I don't mean British Petroleum. It's Bakken Production. I don't know where they have an office in town."

"And what's he drive?"

"What the fuck is up with you. Is this twenty questions or what?"

"It's you being a good guy and me being a good tipper."

"Yeah, right. Anyway, he drives a company truck when he's around here. It's a four door, a crew cab, GMC pickup with a shell on the back."

"Color?"

"Tan, like all BP's equipment."

I wave over my shoulder and head for the van. As soon as I get seated and out of the cold, I check my phone again, and there's another message from Pax, and new coordinates where the red Caddy has again parked.

And I'm off. Isn't it great to be able to follow somebody and never lay eyes on them or their vehicle!

As I drive off, I'm wondering why Speck is meeting with a guy who's fairly high up in the Owens-McKittrick chain of command? Maybe I'm getting a little closer to the head of the snake. I text Pax and give him the name Nickleston and the fact he's a superintendent for Owens-McKittrick. If the guy has a less than stellar background, Pax will find it.

The new coordinates are ten miles closer to town, and I get close, but not quite there, and a locked gate stops my progress. A car has recently driven in, as tracks are fresh. I go ahead and circle what seems to be a section, a mile on each side, but there are no other roads into the place other than that locked gate. On the far side of the section I come across a grove of box elders, and they give way to a long row of cottonwoods that line what is probably a creek in the spring. I carefully work the van off the road and into the box elders a little, just enough that I'm not blocking the little road that's only about two lanes wide between some barbwire fences.

Surviving in the winter, in the snow and ice, is a learned art, and I learned it well at MWTC, the Marine winter training center near Bridgeport, California, high in the Sierras to the east of Yosemite National Park. And the training is rigorous. The bad news about working in the snow, of course the cold can kill you and water is tough to come by, even though you're surrounded by the frozen version. The good news, if you're dressed in white and if you have time to pound the snow down, you're tough to spot and have a foxhole a damn sight easier to create than digging in tough terrain. The worst news; it's impossible not to leave a trail and the trail stays until it snows like hell again.

My Carhartt lined pants are tan, not the best, but my North Face coat is reversible, red on one side and white on the other. So I reverse it. My hat is fur lined and the same tan as my pants. I want to travel light, so I leave the long arms in the van and take only my .40 cal Glock and my binocs. Thank God I'm wearing my one thousand gram Thinsulate boots, as the snow is damn near eighteen inches deep. I work my way over a broken down section of the barbwire fence and head out. Checking my phone, I see it's four forty five. I've got a little over a half hour before sunset, then it really gets cold. The weather man says twenty below is the low. As I trudge toward the GPS coordinates, I'm happy to note that they denote a location on my side of center in the section, I'd guess I've got a three eighths of a mile hike, if I can get close.

I can normally walk a mile in fifteen minutes if I can pick 'em up and put 'em down, but the country is low hills, like most of this part of North Dakota, and the snow is deep. It takes me fifteen minutes to cover a quarter of a mile, but the quarter mile mark seems to be the highest place in the section of land, and I can see structures five hundred yards ahead, not houses, but two metal Quonset hut shaped barns, and smoke is coming from a stack on one of them. About the time I'm feeling sorry for myself out in the cold, I jump a pair of pronghorn antelope who have to leave their beds under a lonely cottonwood out of place near the crown of the hill. I feel a little guilty as I'm sure it takes some time to warm a spot up. Then I feel envious as I wish I could run like that in eighteen inches of snow.

There are two windows in the ends of each of the Quonset huts nearest me and two trucks and the red Caddy are parked at the other end, so I presume the doors into the huts are there.

I quarter to the side away from the windows and move to within a hundred yards, then stomp a flat spot in the snow and settle down and wait for darkness. Even if they were looking right at me, I could duck into my hidey hole and not be seen.

There have been times when I was more confortable. I dig my phone out and play a little solitaire, then get a wild hair and call Jennifer in Vegas. If you've got to kill time, why not do so with a beautiful woman. I do wish I was in her sack and wouldn't wish or her, her being in my snowy hole.

"Hey, I figured you'd run for the hills," she answers.

"Actually, I'm in the hills, so you're not far off."

We talk for fifteen minutes, and as seems to be the daily norm, and thank God for it, the sun sets. I promise to call more often, then ease my eyes over the edge of my hole. And I'm just in time to see the Caddy working it's way around the small parking area, then head out. The two trucks are still there.

In ten more minutes it's dark enough not to be seen, as the moon is not up yet. One of the disadvantages of snow is even the moon can light the landscape enough that you can be spotted.

But I don't have to get next to the buildings to figure out what's going on there.

If a place is not properly insulated, and sometimes even if it is, you can smell a meth lab a mile away— which is a good reason for them to be this remote. I presume these are well insulated, unless built for dry storage only—but still they stink like hell.

I'd like to try and figure out how to light the place up and blow whoever occupies the trucks into the stratosphere, but the object is to cut the head off the snake, not a couple of inches off its tail.

I'm about to haul ass before mine freezes off when I hear a door close. I drop down on my belly and watch as someone moves across the parking lot and climbs into a truck. I raise my binocs so I can get a good look at him as he's only seventy five yards away, and am sure he's missing the lobe of one ear. Luthor, as I recall. I wish I had gotten close enough to GPS rig the two trucks, but I haven't. He hits the lights on the truck and I have to hunker lower in the snow as they bathe me on a swing by.

If they're leaving, and I doubt if all of whomever is inside will go as a meth lab of his size may have millions in product inside, and somebody will stand guard, I could recon the place closer, but decide it's too big a risk, and head out.

Luckily I can follow my own tracks back to the van, and as I do I ask the good Lord to make it snow tonight so my tracks aren't made by the scumbags. I don't want the meth boys to have any suspicion that someone is onto them.

You got to love a warm van when it's already well below zero...well below. But it takes me ten minutes to warm mine up.

The warmth is good, but knowing I'm getting close to the head of this particular snake is even better.

I think it's time to clean up and go back to Big Rosie's as Mike Reardon and see what worms work their way out of the woodwork.

Sometimes you've got to tease the snake to get him out of his hole.

Chapter Nineteen

As soon as I hit the camper, my phone buzzes with an unknown caller. I answer in my normal polite manner. "What?"

"Toby?"

"Who wants to know?"

"Hey, *pendajo*, this is your main man, Big Al."

"Yo, man. What's happening?"

"You wanted to talk about a deal?"

"I checked out okay?"

He laughs lowly. "Yeah, man, you done fucked up plenty. We can do a little biz."

Obviously Pax did a good job building Toby's phony background. "Let's talk. Where?"

"I got to get some chow, how 'bout that Rosie's joint."

"Cool. I got some things going down. An hour okay?"

"I don't wait on nobody."

"I'm always on time."

"Be there," he says, and hangs up. I check the time and see I need to be there by seven thirty, which means the place should be hopping.

I was going to ditch the disguise and use some finger polish remover to get the friggin' beard off, but now I guess I'll need it for a while longer. Pax suggested I take this scumbag escapee from Atascadero State Mental Hospital out hard, so maybe that's exactly what I should do.

It's time to dig into my Wells Cargo trailer and my bag of dirty tricks.

A quarter pound of C4 and two phone activated detonators should solve this little problem.

The parking lot is already full when I arrive in my van. I look the lot over carefully until I find a black Expedition with the right license plate. The C4 and detonator is in a small metal box with a powerful magnet tapped to it, and I check the parking lot for observers, and seeing none place it under the vehicle, on the inside of a frame I-beam, directly under the driver's seat. Guarding against a wrong number that might injure or kill an innocent bystander, Pax has rigged the phone detonator to activate after the answer and only with the input of a four number code by the caller.

I note there's also a candy apple red Caddy in the lot, so I repeat the process and now two assholes are riding eighth of a pound C4 bombs…and before I reach the front door, my phone buzzes again and I see I have a text, 'must be a party, all units converged on Rosie's.' Interesting, all the guys who've cars and trucks I've laid a GPS tracker unit on, are in one place. The ball of slimy snakes are together. I wish I could just blow the whole joint to hell, but there're lots of innocent folks at hand. Oh, well.

This time when I push through the doors I'm greeted by Big and Rich with "…discount box wine burnin' like turpentine, anything to get a buzz," and the place is already rocking. I work my way back to the restaurant area and stop short.

Looks as if there's a little conflict going on. People are moving away from tables as Speck, his bald headed body guard, and five other guys, including Maggy's son Emmitt, Broken Toes, Many Horses, a big dude who looks familiar to me as he has a little Dutch boy's black bangs are lined up facing—with about ten feet separating them—Big Al, Curly, Tamale, the guy called Luthor with the missing ear lobe, the two V boys, and the guy who must be The Bear as he's at least four hundred pounds. They are facing each other like Napoleon and the Duke of Wellington's forces at Waterloo.

Between the two lines is a guy I have yet to get a line on, and he's talking like a Dutch uncle; looks as if he's trying to prevent a war.

His head swivels back and forth like he's watching a tennis match, and his jaw is flapping, and then things seem to ease, and the lines start to break up and move away to opposite sides of the room. I hold tight awhile, watching Big Al until he goes to a large booth in a back corner, and his boys surround him. The others are far away, so I go ahead and approach. Guys who've left their tables begin to filter back and return to their suppers or drinks.

The guy who seemed to be negotiating the peace, joins neither group, but instead heads for the bar and takes a stool.

I walk right up to Big Al, and he eyes me, checks the time on his phone, and says, "You're two fucking minutes late."

"I was here, man. You was busy."

"Yeah, *pendajo*, fucking Indian uprising." Then he and his buddies all laugh. I glance over my shoulder and see the three skanks I met in the trailer and also joining up. It seems they beat a trail when whatever has happening began.

"Let's talk," Big Al says, and pushes one of his Russian buddies out of the way. One of the V's, I'd guess as he has a gym rat's body and is about four inches shorter than I am. He turns back to the huge Russian, who was across the table, The Bear, and snaps, "stay behind, but close behind."

"Da," the big guy mumbles and forces his way

"Come on, *pendajo*" he says, and waves me after him as he heads for the door.

I follow, and note that one of the V's and The Bear are trailing forty feet behind.

He leads me straight to the Expedition, waves me around to the passenger seat, climbs in on top of a quarter pound of C4, and checks me out before speaking. "You carrying?" he asks.

"Fuck yes."

He shrugs. "How much you think you can deal?"

"I haven't tested the market, but I got some ins with a couple of the big companies doing biz in the patch."

"Who?" he asks.

"Dawson Personnel, the big placement guys, and Owens-McKittrick."

He laughs. "That Okie fuck Speck has Owens-McKittrick all tied up, or thinks he does, but if you can work it, be my guest. We don't need any help with Dawson."

"Then Owens-McKittrick it is. I got buddies in all the camps—"

"Who?"

"Me to know…if you had buddies in all the camps you wouldn't need me."

He laughs again. "How many o's?" I'm testing him to see if he really is a major dealer.

"Fuck ounces, about five kilos."

He eyes me carefully. "Five bricks. How long to get it laid off."

I shrug. "A week, maybe less."

"You got five grand?"

"You checked me out. How about I pay when I pick up the next five."

"Fuck that," he says. "That's half the street value. You can pick up an easy ten. You got no dough?"

"I got some. How about some crank or brown?"

"Get rid of the five bricks. I'll let you owe me twenty five hun, but you'll go in a hole in the ice you don't pay up in a week."

"I got two grand." I lie, but it sounds good to this crumb bum.

"Then you get four bricks and will owe me two more."

"Done," I say, and bump fists with him.

"When will you have the dough?"

"I got it in my rig now."

He climbs out of the Expedition and waves the small Russian over. "Go check on the girls, then head out and pick up four bricks. Slick here will lay two g's on you and hand them over."

The Russian eyes me carefully, and with a croaking voice points across the highway. "That parking lot over there at the tan building. I'll be there in one and a half hours. Be there, with cash."

I nod, and the Russian gets in the Caddy and the three of us head back to the front door. Before we hit it, he turns to me. "You go in the back way. We don't meet up no more. Got it?"

"I got it. Fine by me." As I'm moving around the building, I text Pax. 'Track the Expedition carefully for a stop. Heading 4 their warehouse.'

As I'm now persona non grata, I head for the bar, and run into Rosie's big boss, Paul Feldman. He's leaning on the wall near his office door, which seems to be a place he favors. I would speak to him, but he doesn't know me as a scraggly blond with a goatee. Neither does Maggy, the bartender on this end of the busy bar, so I get a beer without her spitting in it.

I'm halfway through the beer when I turn to survey the crowd, and am surprised to see Detective DiAngelo and the beautiful copper blond Amber amble in and move near the dance floor and find a table. I watch them a moment, then realize they're not happy with each other.

As I'm studying them, kind of catch and catch can as four couples on the dance floor are between us, I'm surprised by someone laying a hand on my shoulder, and glance up to see the big Indian with the black bangs, glaring at me, his grip on my shoulder is not friendly.

"Do I know you?" he asks, and I remember exactly where I've seen him. He was the asshole with the wasp spray.

"You're gonna know me way better than you want to, you don't get that fucking paw off my shoulder."

"Tough guy, uh," he says with a grin that covers his foot wide face, showing yellow teeth. But he removes the hand.

"How about Attica," I ask. "You do some time in Attica. You a Pequot? Or a Mohawk?"

"What the fuck's a Pequot," he asks, looking puzzled.

"It's a fucking Indian, Indian," I say, "from north of New York."

"Them eastern Indians is all pussys," he snarls, and I shrug.

"I guess we don't know each other then," I say, and give him my back and go back to my beer, and he moves on along with three others from Speck's group—Speck, Big John Broken Toes, and Albert Many Horses—and they head out the back door.

Even over the music, I hear the slap that Amber lays on her table mate. To DiAngelo's credit he doesn't slap her back, but catches the other wrist as she tries for a double. Then she jumps up and heads for the front door. He's red in the face, maybe from the slap, but for sure from pure anger.

I intercept her. I can see DiAngelo on his feet by the table, and raise my voice a little. "I'll walk her out."

I can see him calm a little, and then nod. He knows, as I know, that no beautiful woman should be in Rosie's parking lot alone at night. But he's too pissed at her to be her guardian, and she doesn't want him to be.

She's spitting mad as we go through the front doors.

"You okay?" I ask.

"Fine. Good thing I brought my own car." She slips a little on the icy pavement, and I caution her, with a hand on her upper arm to steady her.

"Where is it?" I ask, but she doesn't answer, just charges on, and I follow her across the lot, then catch up and grab her arm again and stop her as the creep Speck and his three soldiers move out from between cars, and stand waiting for us…and every one of them is holding a hand out of sight behind a thigh. My adrenaline is starting to surge. I grab my phone and eyeball it, hitting the voice record app, then return it to my coat pocket and turn to the lady.

Speck laughs. "911 ain't gonna help you."

"Go back inside," I say over my shoulder to Amber.

"No way." She says, the anger still palpable in her tone.

She starts down between the a car and truck, but Broken Toes starts to fade the same way three cars in front of us, and I can see that she sees his movement, and her eyes flare a little.

"Hold up, Amber," I caution, and she stops and glances back, this time a twitch of fear registers near her eyes.

"What's your problem, Charmin?" I say to Speck, a little growl in my voice.

"Charming? You a queer or something?"

"I didn't say charming, I said Charmin…as in butt wipe."

"Fuck you," he snaps, then asks, "You working with Two Cents?" His voice is low and a little ominous.

"Who the fuck is Two Cents and who's asking?" I know, but don't want him to know I know.

He cuts his eyes to Amber. "That a new bitch?" he says, smiling as if he knows how far off base he is.

I turn to the side a little like I'm saying something to her, and ease a hand to my back, and to the Glock, then glance back at him. "Let's let the lady get in her car and get out of here and we'll talk all you want."

"She's fine gash," he says, an evil grin, "maybe I can trade your bitch for three Russian bitches."

"Run, back to Tony," I say in a low voice to Amber, but instead she starts slipping back my way between the cars, now with fear in her eyes.

Speck moves a little closer, and Amber comes until she's half behind me.

"Harold here," Speck motions to the guy with the black bangs, "says you're the same guy who was here a couple of weeks ago, but you changed your looks. You some undercover fuck or what?"

I turn enough so I'm sure Amber hears me. This time I'm adamant. "Get back in the restaurant." But she seems frozen in place.

So I answer Speck. "He's crazy, and I'm from Nevada."

"How about we kick the shit out of you and send you back to Nevada, maybe in a body bag," he says, and takes a couple of steps forward as do his buddies. Now they show what they have in their hands, three of them have eighteen inch lengths of pipe, and Speck has a large pistol.

That's bad news. The good news, I have a large pistol…not quite as large as his, but large enough and probably with twice as many cartridges. And I'm not taking a chance on them getting lucky…I might not wake up in the hospital this time, or ever again.

Speck's pistol has a hammer on the semi-auto, probably a 1911 .45, and I hear him ratchet it back as he says, "Fuck him up," to his buddies, and they charge.

I'm squeezing the trigger as I whip the Glock out and bring the muzzle up at Speck, with the pistol being the number one threat, and the first shot takes him through the groin and a hip bone I presume, as it spins him like a whirling dervish. All three of the others drop back in shock, and I'm not surprised in the least when the pipes hit the ground and they're digging into coat pockets and holsters on hips. I catch black bangs dead center between his tits and he reels back, eyes rolled up, wind milling his arms; but it's a pity I went for him and didn't double tap Speck as from flat on his back his .45 is spitting flame, and roaring like the canon it is. The other two Indians are ducking between cars and trucks as I am, firing wildly as the run and bullets are cutting the air all around us like hornets on the hunt. While I'm trying to get some cover from a CJ4 that's to my right.

I put two more into Speck and he jerks like he was hit with 220 volts, then turn my attention to the other two, as black bangs is flat on his back and not moving. I need to make sure the other two are not just seeking cover behind vehicles.

Light flares in the parking lot and I look over my shoulder to see DiAngelo running from the front door of Rosie's. He slides up beside me, and almost loses his balance, then I think he does as he goes down, but he's merely kneeling.

"Who?" he says, and looks up at me with pure fury in his eyes, and only then do I realize that Amber has taken one in the chest, and maybe the same one that's singed my arm badly as it roared by. My stomach sinks and bile rises in my throat, then it goes so dry I can barely speak.

"Four of them," I croak. "I got two down, two to go."

"Where," he says between clinched teeth, and I point the way they went, and he leaves as quickly as a man can move on an icy parking lot. "Call 911," he yells over his shoulder as he moves away.

But I don't bother to make the call. Nothing will help Amber, and I see bystanders nearby on their phones. As the parking lot starts to fill with people filtering out of the saloon, I pop the clip on the Glock and ratchet the shell in the chamber out, locking the slide open so the cops arriving can see it's no threat, and I can hear the sirens coming. I set on my butt on the icy parking lot, and put Amber's head in my lap, and whisper, "I'm so, so sorry," and wait. It's been a long time since my eyes have filled with tears.

Revenge does a slow creep up my backbone, and I know it won't go away until I spill the blood of those who were part of the cause.

The hell of it is, I was also part.

All of these assholes, all of these fucking dope dealers and pimps, are not worth this one beautiful lady. And I'm not either.

But the fact is, we got some snakes out of the their hole...now to roust the others.

Chapter Twenty

I don't see DiAngelo again until he walks into the interview room where I've been answering questions for three hours. Two detectives and the Chief of Police are across the table from me when he sticks his head in.

"You do any good?" I ask.

"No. You didn't do worth a shit either."

"That's a pure fact," I say, and it's all I can do not to hang my head in shame.

"I'll be at my desk when these guys finish with you. I'm buying breakfast."

I nod, and he starts to leave, and I call after him, "Hey, man, you have no idea how sorry I am."

"Ain't we all," he says over his shoulder as he moves away.

They bring in mug books and I look for the two guys who left the scene at a run, then suggest they call the Rez police and get pics of Broken Toes and Many Horses. I have better pics of them than the cops do, then realize that Pax has probably emailed them to DiAngelo by now, and inform them of that and one of the detectives leaves, and returns in a few minutes and advises the chief that they're being printed now. They're interested in how and why I have pics, and why I know these guys, and I explain that I'm working for an undisclosed client as a private security guy. That takes an hour to work through with lots of threats on their part. But I, of course, hold firm on my non-disclosure.

Finally the chief eyes me carefully, then asks, "Who the fuck are you...really."

"Just a guy who does a little security work, chief."

"You knocked off half the cartel in Vegas, or so the word is. You dusted off two really bad boys tonight, both of whom were carrying, and ran two more off. And it's not often we get a voice recording of a crime in process." I've emailed the audio file off my phone to them, which is one of the reasons they're being easy on me. He continues, "That's not the work of some security guy."

I shrug, and smile a little wanly. "Sometimes I get a little pissed. When do I get my Glock back?"

He shakes his head. "If that's a 'little pissed' I'd hate to see you get really mad. Your Glock is part of an ongoing investigation, as you well know. Besides, if you're who you seem to be, and have done half of what's coming in on you over the wire, you got plenty of weapons laying around."

"Not me. I'll have to find a store and buy another pistol for self-protection."

"Right." He's on his feet, and speaks to the two dicks at the table. "Get him another cup of coffee. Go over his story one more time, then let DiAngelo buy his breakfast." He shakes his head a little disgustedly, then adds, "The prick's never bought my breakfast, and I sign his checks."

"Thanks, chief," I say as he heads for the door. "Take good care of my Glock."

He waves over his shoulder and is gone.

And we start though the story again.

It's bar closing time by the time they cut me loose, but DiAngelo, as promised, is still at his desk. He stands as I approach. "We have an APB out on Broken Toes and Many Horses but no sign of them yet. Let's go eat." He leads the way to the department parking. Which is fine as I rode in with a detective. He motions me to a plain clothes vehicle, and as we climb in says, "We've got to go to the truck stop as it's the best of what's open now. You're wheels are still at Rosie's?"

"Far as I know, if some prick hasn't stolen them."

He sits quiet for a moment before he turns the key over, and sighs deeply as the oatmeal colored Chevy fires up in the cold, then offers, "I'll drop you off there. I listened to the tape about ten times. You really tried to get her out of it, didn't you?"

"Several times. But it wouldn't have happened had I not had trouble with those assholes. She got caught up in something she sure as hell didn't deserve."

He starts the car and pulls out of the lot before he continues and his voice catches as he speaks, "Fate's…fate's a friggin' hunter."

I can't help but ask, "What were you fighting about?"

"Makes me sick to think of it. I met her as she came out of work and asked her to supper at Pop's place, ordered a bottle of his best Champagne, and she thought I was going to propose. I wish I had…even under the circumstance." He lets that lie and I don't ask, and he continues, "I laughed when she said so as we left, and she got pissed…really pissed. Nothing like a woman scorned. Anyway, I took her to her office where I'd picked her up after work so she could get her car, then as

Rosie's was not too far, talked her into having a drink with me."

"Sounds like she was cooling off," I offer.

"She was, then, right after we sat down, I leveled with her and confessed that I never finalized my divorce from my first marriage and couldn't get legally married if I wanted to. She flipped out and cracked me a good one across the chops and hauled ass."

We're both quiet for a while as he drives, seemingly far away in thought, then he asks as we pull into the Flying J truck stop, "You got any idea where those assholes might be holing up?"

"Truthfully, I didn't have my buddy email you quite all the stuff I had."

"You were holding out?"

"Yeah, a couple of things, one of which is a place that might just be a good hide out for a couple big-as-a-bull fuckheads who deserve to die."

He stops short. "Why hold out?"

"Because the way I do biz might not set well with Williston PD, and I don't like to see assholes like those two get accessory to murder at twenty five to life and out in eight while Amber is…" I start to say rotting in a grave, but think twice, and instead say, "…is cold and gone."

"I get that," he says. "You think you hate it, try being a cop with today's judges and today's packed prisons." We find a booth in a far corner, away from any possible prying ears.

He smiles tightly at me. "When are we going after them?"

"We being you and a swat team?"

He shakes his head no. Then says, in a low voice, "Nope, we being you and I and I don't much give a shit how it comes down. Let's just go with the flow and take them as they come, and I mean take them...."

"How about after we chow down?"

He nods. "I hate to kill a couple of fucking lowlife scumbags on an empty stomach."

I'm starting to like Detective Tony DiAngelo like he was a brother. He even buys breakfast as promised.

As we leave, I insist, "You got to take me to my van before we head out to the country."

"They won't recognize this Chevy."

"Yeah, but you don't know what I carry in the van."

Chapter Twenty One

He eyes me with interest, then nods and says, "The van it is."

As we head for his car, I am not just a little surprised to see a familiar face. How many girls would be out in twenty below weather, flashing open a down coat that hangs to her ankles, showing a pair of orange hot pants over yellow tights, with hair now bright orange contrasting nicely with her very dark skin. She's headed for the coffee shop, slipping and sliding across the icy parking lot, a red wool scarf wrapped around her face up to the eyes and over her head like she's a Muslim maiden.

"Vanna?" I call out, and she stops short and almost goes on her butt.

"Who dat?" she asks, and moves closer.

"You remember me. We met at the truck stop in Billings."

"I meets lots of boys," she says, and giggles.

"How's tricks?"

"Super, but I'd rather be in Billings or heading sout'. I 'bout to freeze my titties off. You knows what I mean?"

"What brought you back?"

143

"Man came got me."

She's been looking down, but glances up and I can see a puffed eye. "Speck punch you?" I ask.

"Yeah, he da daddy…but de send the dat fat prick Emmitt to get me. He done punched me."

"Did he hurt you bad…anything other than the black eye?"

"Been peeing some blood. Gots to go to the head."

I call after her as she hurries away, "I gotta go, but I'll be back." I pull a Repairman card out of my wallet, nothing but a phone number to an answering device owned by Pax and an email address routed through India and Malta, and hustle after her and hand it to her. "Vanna, you call me. I'm gonna help you get where it's warm."

She nods and smiles, and I think but don't say, and you're gonna help me get rid of a bunch of Russian scum.

"Let's get it done," Tony yells, and I hustle to the Chevy.

As soon as I get seated I go to my iPhone and look up the recents on Driving Directions and get the route started again. As we drive out to the northeast, to the old farmhouse where Pax had tracked Speck's phone, I try to make sense of the mess of bad guys, and know it'll help if I bounce it off someone else, and who knows what DiAngelo knows that he has yet to share.

So I start to ramble. "Speck I met when I first walked in Rosie's. He was with some big bald dude who we haven't made—"

"Augie Romanski. I've got a folder on him. He's nothing but dumb muscle, but he carries a cannon, one of those .50 cal monstrosities."

"Then I tangled up with the Indians, and this guy, Emmitt, Maggy the bartender's son."

He laughs, and cuts his eyes to me as he drives. "Yeah, I got the word you busted his nose and creased the skull of his two Indian buddies."

"The assholes were trying to bust into my trailer, right in the parking lot at Rosie's. And then I stumbled into the boy in the Jesus Loves Me bus, Curly, and his two buddies, Al and Tamale. To be truthful, I think my employer had a good idea that some bad shit was going down where it was suggested..." I don't tell him that Owens-McKittrick was paying my rent on one of their properties... "...suggested that I stay where I'm parking my camper."

"I know exactly where you're parked and who else is resident on that lot."

I shrug. "Good for you. Anyway, then there's the Russians this guy Al, Two Cents is his nickname, is tied up with."

"Two Cents, how'd you find that out? We haven't been able to make the guy."

"A bad, bad boy who escaped from Atascadero State Mental Hospital in California. You can pick him up anytime...but the world would be a better place if he pulled a gun on someone who was legally carrying, like you or I, and the state was spared the expense of a trial and three hots and cot for the rest of his days."

He merely nods, and by the way his jaw clamps I'm sure he agrees totally. Then he asks, "What got him locked in the loony bin?"

"Rape and murder, in the worst way. One of his rape vics was over seventy years old."

"Too bad about him getting the shit shot out of him," he says, again shaking his head.

"Yeah, too bad, now to actually make it happen." His jaw clamps even tighter and I can see he means to make it happen. So I hope to bring it all together, and ask, "Anyway so how does this all tie in?"

"And it does, at least I'm starting to put it together. The Indians, led by Speck who's a white-eye, rent girls from the Russians and the Russians buy dope, Mexican brown, marijuana and coke, wholesale from the Indians, who have ties all the way to Mexico. And the Ruskies manufacture Meth somewhere nearby. They are at odds, but they need each other. The Indians and the Russians have the town and the counties around divided up, the Indians have everything south of 15th, the Russians everything north. And they have separated the counties into territories. There's a guy, a guy with a twisted arm, and he is in place with the Indians, put there by the Russians, to watch them. The Indians know exactly what's going on, and put up with him. You don't seen him hanging with them, but he's around during any major transaction He's the Ruskies eye-in-the-sky. And he's a bad son of a bitch...we think he's the Russians major enforcer. His nickname is Lobo."

I'm nodding my head as it seems to make sense.

"So, what was the big conflict in Rosie's all about?"

"A couple of the Russians, that big ugly fuck they call the Bear and one they call Vasily, beat the crap out of the girl we checked out in the morgue, and she was on duty for the Indians at the time, and they recruited her out of Seattle. It was a minor spat as far as all those pricks are concerned. I've got a CI who hangs at Rosie's and got him aside after I failed in my pursuit and returned to the parking lot. He says there's a major meeting somewhere tomorrow afternoon...late."

I nod my head, knowingly, and he asks, "Okay, someplace else you didn't mention?"

"Yeah, a couple of Quonset huts in the middle of a section of snow covered fallow ground. There's a major meth operation there. It's on top of my hit list."

"Okay, now we're getting somewhere."

"What do you have on a suit, a guy who's a field superintendent for Bakken Production...name of Nickleston?"

"Never heard of the guy."

"Speck met with him for a nice long private talk out of earshot of others. I'm waiting for some background on the guy."

"I'll be interested."

My van, thank God, is in Rosie's parking lot where it was left, setting cold and lonely covered with new fallen snow.

I invite DiAngelo in the back and he sits on my narrow bunk while I go to the cabinet over my tiny sink and find the two levers that allow it to swing away from the panel behind, where a pair of fully automatic Colt M4's await. This is the same rifle I carried in Iraq, except these two have been modified even more than the original was from the M16. The weapon is only thirty three inches with the stock fully extended, and these are configured so the stock folds away. That and a shortened barrel, from fourteen and a half inches to seven and a quarter inches, only a half inch in front of the foresight, leaving just enough to thread for suppressors, make it little more than an auto pistol. She's not as good beyond two hundred yards as she once was, but great in tight quarters. Under where DiAngelo sits is a long reaching .308 semi-auto sniper rifle for distance work, a SASS or semi auto sniper system, but I doubt if that'll be needed tonight as the snow will inhibit any long distant shooting, even with the night vision scope.

The M4's both have combat lights mounted on the muzzles and Sightmark battle sights for quick target acquisition.

He whistles like he's eying a long legged blond when I hand one over. "Fully auto," I say, then reach back into the hidey hole behind the cabinet and fish out two canvas bags, each holding six thirty-shot clips, which have been taped together in twos, and I hand him one of those as well. "Don't hold the trigger down, at almost a thousands rounds a minute you'll eat up those hundred eighty rounds in a couple of heartbeats. I point at the rapid fire switch, suggest you set her for three round bursts."

"I wish we had these at the department," he says, eyeing the weapon with some admiration.

I dig into the cabinet under the sink and hit another pair of tiny levers and the side pops open, revealing another hide out spot. I hand him a pair of grenades. "Flash grenades. They'll give us a few second advantage if we have to charge in after these pricks."

"Those I've used," he says.

"You got extra clips for your sidearm?" I ask, as I recover a combat thigh holster for mine, and strap it on.

"Two, each with fifteen, plus a fifteen shot clip in the weapon, and one in the hole."

"Great, me too. You ready to rock and roll?"

Chapter Twenty Two

I can see the determination in DiAngelo's dark eyes. "I've been ready, now I'm even more ready."

We've got a twenty mile drive, and drive it in silence. It's snowing lightly and he's having to pay attention to the road. "How much farther?" he asks.

I check the driving directions on my phone. "Two miles, you still up for this? Chances are this playbook is not in the Williston PD good-cop manual."

"I guess if there are no witnesses except those of us who are culpable, the playbook is what we say it is."

"I doubt if we'll want to hang around to have to explain anything...if that works for you."

"Anything about what? I'm home in the sack getting my beauty rest. And I dropped you off to pick up your van after we'd talked a couple of hours."

"Just in case there's anyone inside who's innocent, who stays alive, I've got full face ski masks, and suggest you wear one. Wouldn't want you to get frostbite...or recognized."

"I've got a knit cap in my pocket, but full face is way better."

I dig under my seat, and next to the tire spikes I use to throw out behind me and flatten tires in case I'm being pursued, I find the facemasks and hand one over.

But I keep up the caution. "If we walk away from this, and don't get back to the trailer, these two beautiful weapons will have to find a resting place at the bottom of the Muddy River. We throw a lot of brass and don't want it to come back to us."

"That we can do," he says. "But why only if we don't get back to your trailer."

"I got wise and have extra barrels for them, new barrels, new markings on the bullets. They might tie the casings, but what kind of proof is it if the bullets don't match? The snow's getting worse…good, it's good cover."

In another few minutes, we're at the gate, which again is locked with a simple master lock, and again, under the headlights of the van, I quickly pick it.

I climb back into the driver's seat, and as we pull away, Tony asks, "I presume you were a B and E man before you went in the Corps?"

"I've picked a few locks in my time…all for good reason, of course."

"Of course," he repeats, then I hear the bolt being thrown on the M4, and caution him, "You know where the safety is?"

"Yep," he answers.

I pull off the two track driveway before we reach the crest of the hill where we can be seen from the barn. I nose the van off, then back up so we're facing back the way we came, turn off the headlights, and back up and over the crest.

"Let's check this out," I suggest and stop and we dismount and walk to what's now the back of the van, facing downhill.

But the falling snow is thick enough that we can't make out the barn, and see no lights.

"It's two hundred yards or so to the barn. Let's get a hundred yards closer, then go in on foot."

"Works for me," he says, then asks, "Are we going in or shall we try and lure them out?"

"Let's let the quality of the lock on the door help determine that. And I've got another trick you might not have seen."

"Okay, Houdini. Lay it on me."

I hold up my iPhone.

He shrugs. "So, an iPhone...."

"Yeah, but did you ever hear of the FLIR One?"

"Flyer?"

"Nope, this is a heat sensing app, and small hardware, as you can see, that wraps the iPhone much like a spare battery case, a visible-spectrum camera much like the very high end ones the Military uses...and this one's been ramped up by my tech buddies and is even more sensitive. The good news, it's not forty grand or even four, it's more like three hundred fifty bucks."

"So, we can see through the walls?"

I laugh low, and am straining to see as I back closer to the barn. "Well, you can't peek on the girls in the locker room, but you can outline warm bodies, particularly if they're close to the outside walls. Not only that, you can video record the session. It was actually developed for uses like detecting insulation leaks...it's good for a one tenth degree difference in temperature detection."

"Amazing."

"If you can thunk it, someone somewhere can dunk it."

He's ready, even eager. "Let's put it to work."

We're a hundred yards away, and I can only make out an outline of the structure in the snow occluded moonlight.

I motion to him and show him that I've placed the keys under the drivers seat, and we're out in the cold and moving toward the barn. Two vehicles are parked near the big double doors in front of the barn, and I can make out a couple more near the rear, but have no idea make and model, or even color as all are white, snow covered.

I speak as low as possible to be heard over the wind, which is beginning to moan a little as the snow is getting thicker. "You watch our six. I'll have to concentrate on the screen."

Switching on the unit, we begin to slowly work our way along the length of the building, letting the FLIR do it's work. I make out nothing, then pull up and study the screen as I'm getting a bright red image.

"Somebody?" Tony whispers.

"No, a water heater."

It's about a hundred feet on the long side walls of the barn, and maybe the building is fifty or sixty feet wide. Just after we pass the mid point where the water heater was seen, I get another reading, and this time I think it's human. I show Tony the long horizontal reading, about bed height from the floor.

He smiles tightly. "Some big fat fuck...I'm surprised we can't hear him snoring, or snortin' like a hippo."

We move on and in six feet get another reading. And he smiles again. "Another big som'bitch. I think we've scored.

But we're not through, as we near the end we spot two more, one I'd guess at only five feet in length, one just a little longer, probably working girls the boys have stashed here. Then I realize they're stacked…bunk beds, and there are two sets next to the outside walls.

As we turn the corner at the rear of the barn, we see two more vehicles, and I walk to one I think I recognize and wipe the snow away enough to see, even in the dim light, a candy apple red color. I'm pretty sure Speck is in the morgue as I saw the meat wagon haul him off from Rosie's parking lot…so one of the other dipshits must have driven it here.

I think we've hit the jackpot.

There's another pair of vehicle size barn doors on this end as well, but there's also a passage door. The barn doors seem to be barred from the inside as there's no lock, yet they're immobile. And the passage door is the Hollywood type with window in the top half. It's locked, but rather than pick it, and with the wind now howling and my hand's gloved, I go ahead and break the glass, reach in, and the lock pops when I turn the inside knob.

We stand quiet for a moment, just on the slight chance we've been heard. But nothing.

"Let's move," Tony says over my shoulder, and I shove the door open.

The alarm clangs loud enough to wake the dead in the next county, and doesn't stop.

Chapter Twenty Three

We bust inside at a run, panning our combat lights from side to side, then realize that to our left is a line of horse stalls, at least eight from front to back, but on the right, with a twenty foot aisle separating them, is a line of rooms. The one nearest our end is much the largest, if the spacing of the doors is any indicator.

"Cover in the stalls," I yell to Tony, who moves to the fourth stall and vaults the railings while I do the same in the second. And we don't have to wait long as the alarm goes off, a light appears under the second door, the second door bursts open, light floods the aisle from that room, and some very big boy in a coat, no pants, and pull on snow boots stumbles out. He has a pump shotgun in one hand and a handheld floodlight in the other. I've turned my muzzle mounted combat light off, but Tony hasn't, and the guy swings the light Tony's way, just as the door fills with another big boy, also with a weapon in hand, the first one pumps a shell in as he's raising the muzzle to follow his light.

We fire at the same time, the boy with the shotgun and I, muzzle flashes light the big barn like disco strobes, as I put a quick burst in him, then into the dark doorway with the second burst, but the second guy has faded back out of sight. I presume he's not hit as the light in the room goes out.

The first guy slams back against the doorjamb, then falls slowly tumbles on his face, unmoving.

And there is at least one additional guy in the room, as I hear at least two shouting back and forth. Then the door to that room slams shut.

And the first door opens as I turn my combat light back on, and realign the muzzle to a new threat...but it is women, as I suspected. The girl in the doorway, in a robe with bare feet, and two looking over her shoulder, are wide eyed.

I blind them with my muzzle mounted combat light and yell, "Get back inside and get down." And that door slams as well.

A burst from the shotgun went Tony's way, so I quickly move to his stall, and yell, "Coming your way," and get there to see him on his feet, but picking splinters out of his face.

"Thought I was shot," he says, and gives me a stupid grin, then growls, "kill the light, you're blinding me," and I redirect the light and my muzzle back to the second room and sweep down the bank of rooms making sure no other doors are opening. Then kill my light again.

"One down," I say as he works a slider on the stall door and this time walks out. "And at least two to go."

"The first door opened for a second," he says.

"Women, as we thought. At least that's all I saw."

"Then let's hit the second door."

I nod, however I'm sure in the darkness he can't see, then add, "I'll open, you throw, then I'll go in first."

"Fuck you, me first. You got yours."

"Okay, I'll open, you throw, and after the blast you go first."

"Cool," he says. The first guy is only half blocking the doorway, but his shotgun is still within his reach. I pop the light on and off quick enough to locate it, grab it up, and spin it across the aisle and under the railing of one of the stalls. He's staring into space, and dead, if I ever saw dead. We put our backs to the wall on either side of the door, and I'm happy to note they haven't locked it, and pop it open and drop even farther back, and it's a good thing I do as an automatic stitches holes in the wallboard where I was leaning. Tony throws the flash grenade, and we both turn away, and in a count of three, the room lights up like the New Mexico desert when Fat Boy, our first atomic weapon, exploded and changed the world.

It's time for us to rock the world of whoever is inside, and Tony goes in, firing indiscriminately at anything looking human in the glare of his combat light, with four quick bursts.

There's nothing left for me to do, I realize, hearing nothing in return but moans, and I find the wall switch and turn on an overhead light at the same time sweep the room with the muzzle.

Amber is partially avenged.

Big John Broken Toes is on his back on the cold concrete floor, stitched with 5.56's from his belly to his throat, and he's not gurgling. Emmitt Radiston is on his back, on a bunk, holding his belly and moaning, he's also been hit in a thigh. He was not present when Amber was killed, so I cross the room, jerk his belt off, and put a tourniquet on near his crotch, and it seems to stem the flow of blood.

"What the fuck are you doing," Tony asks.

"He wasn't there when Amber was shot. But we're not through. We got two more doors, plus who knows who's in the room with the ladies."

"We'll get 'em," Tony snaps, "…but this guy's a fucking witness."

"So are the women, and we're not doing them. They can haul his ass out, if he lives."

Speaking of hauling, I reach in his pants pockets and get a set of car keys, cross the room, search for the same with Broken Toes, but find none, then step back to the door and am going through Albert Many Horses pockets when a door at the far end of the barn slides open and a guy's outlined, and a shotgun in his hands roars. With the quick glance I get I recognize the short stocky body with the oddly twisted arm on one side of his body, as he pauses in the doorway and fires…I hit the ground, and the shotgun roars again and pellets cut the air over my head, and Tony ducks back into the room. It's the guy they call Lobo, the one seldom seen.

As I lower the weapon, and push my way back to my feet, another guy sprints out of the darkness and through the door...a very big bald guy, a full head taller than the first, Speck's body guard. He lets fly with a couple of rounds from the .50 cal pistol he carries, and it lights up the room with four foot long muzzle blasts and reverberates the place even more than the shotgun.

The door on the far end of the barn is an easy target but I'm not fast enough as I was using the rifle to push my way to me feet.

"Fuck," Tony says, and busts by me and runs to the other end of the barn seventy five feet away, and I'm on my feet and after him. We both exit the barn carefully, into the blowing snow, and I check for tracks and see that the guys have rounded the barn and are heading back to the far end. We sprint after them and get there just in time to see the candy apple Caddy's tail lights disappearing into the snowstorm.

"Goddamn it, damn it, damn it," Tony yells in frustration.

"Don't sweat it. Watch this act," I say, and pull my iPhone out of my coat pocket and dial a number, then punch in a code, my birthday. "Keep watching," I say.

Just as the Caddy crests the hill behind the barn, maybe three hundred yards from where we stand, the whole world lights up and in the explosive flash we see the Caddy lift off the ground, do a one and a half in the air and land on it's roof, then see it again as it explodes, lighting up the world almost as bright as the first time and begins to burn.

"Jesus J. Christ," Tony mumbles. "I don't know how the fuck you did that, but good work and it sure as hell solves that problem," Tony says.

I have to chuckle. "Don't thank me, thank the Marine Corps demolition class at Pendleton."

But he doesn't brother, he's still out for blood "Let's see who's in the ladies room."

I follow him back inside through the Hollywood door and he moves to the first door that the ladies peeked from.

We flank it, and I reach out and try the knob. It's locked.

"Me first," I say, and he looks disgusted, but nods.

I show him that I have a flash grenade in hand, and he moves back from the door as I cock a foot and boot the door off it's hinges. I toss the grenade in and scramble to the side. Again the count of three, the room does a Fat Boy light up, and we charge in, panning the room with the combat lights,…we see nothing but women.

A dozen women.

And the crescendo of their cries hurts my ears. I walk over and flip on the light to see them piled against the wall at the end of the room, shuddering, wailing. Some of them look even younger than fifteen.

"This must be the hooker wannabe dorm room," Tony says.

"Or more likely the human trafficking supermarket."

"But they looked out the door earlier. It's not like they were being held prisoner."

I nod, "Maybe, maybe not. Where would you go in this snow in your high heels?"

He concedes. "That's a good point."

One of the women steps forward. And in decent, but accented, English asks, "Are you going to kill us?"

"Why," I reply through the ski mask, she can't see my smile, "have you done something to deserve killing?"

She shakes her head rapidly.

"Good, there's a man in the next room who might live if you get him to a hospital." I hand her the keys from the pockets of one of the two dead guys and from Emmitt's. It's a little hard to let a guy die when you've met his mother, even if she wants your balls floating in a martini glass. "You have two minutes to get outside, load up, and get the hell out of here."

She turns and in rapid Russian, yells at the other girls, who begin scrambling around, dragging on the warmest of what they have, and in minutes are out the door. I yell after her. "Get the wounded guy," and she grabs two of the girls and in moments they're stumbling toward Hollywood door, looking strained as hell, with one of Emmitt's meaty arms across their shoulders.

Tony and I go from room to room, making sure no one is left in the place, then from stall to stall and discover bales straw, and behind them are bails of bricks of marijuana, more than two tons worth, I'd guess, as well as several kilos of coke and God knows what else.

I walk back to the Hollywood door and watch the car that had been parked beside the Caddy follow another that they must have gotten from the front of the place, head out the back way. They're hauling ass, slipping and sliding on the road that's now almost a foot deep in snow.

One of the stalls on the front end of the row is a makeshift shop, and inside it is a small generator, and beside the generator is a five gallon can of gas.

I yell to Tony. "Let's make this end then get the hell out of here."

He nods, and I grab the gas can and start spreading fuel over the bales of straw.

"You got a match," I yell at him.

"Don't smoke," he says.

"Check the pockets of the Indians. Both of them smoke like they are sending signals back to the rez."

He does, and in moments is back beside me with a lighter.

"Haul ass to the van," he says, and I need no convincing.

Just as I hit the opening where the front sliding doors have been left open, I hear a "swoosh" and suddenly my shadow is cast in front of me.

"Fuck, run," I hear behind me, but I'm already picking them up and putting them down.

We're half way back to town, enjoying the warmth of the van and some Katy Perry on the Sirius when we see the taillights of the girl's cars in front of us. I'm happy to slow down and let them lead me through the storm back to civilization.

As we drive Tony continues to pick splinters out of bleeding holes in his face and neck. We're lucky its not buckshot, in fact we're lucky we both have heads.

All considered, not a bad night's work. I glance at my watch to check the time, and see the date. Tomorrow's Christmas Eve. I hope we can give the world a present, and get a few more assholes out of the gene pool.

Chapter Twenty Four

It's too damn early when I hear a loud rap on my camper door. I pull on some boxers and peek out to see the two detectives from Williston PD who grilled me for hours, and open up.

"You guys start early," I say. "Not much room, but come on in out of the cold."

The don't sit.

"Late night for you?" One of them asks.

"A little, hit DiAngelo up for breakfast and didn't get in until after three."

"You sure it wasn't about dawn?" he asks.

"Nope, just after three."

The second one says, his tone accusing, "Not much snow on that van outside."

I shrug. "I guess it didn't snow much between three and..." I pick up my phone and see it's eight thirty. "...and eight thirty. Is it snowing now?"

"No."

"Well, there you are. I'd offer you guys a cup of coffee, but none made yet."

The first one snarls, "So you didn't take a trip a few miles northeast of town after you had breakfast?"

"Curled up in my jammies just after three, right there in that sack."

"Looks to me like you sleep in your boxers."

I decide to act a little disgusted. "I haven't had my eight hours of beauty sleep yet. I'll be happy to drop by the station this afternoon if you guys want to continue to have this homo conversation about how I sleep."

"Fuck you, Reardon," one of them says, and leads the other one out the door without bothering with a bye bye, and they go to the bus next door, I'm sure to see if anyone can testify to what time my van pulled in. Fat chance of getting any info out of Curly and the skank, if the cops can even wake them...I'm sure, as usual, they're floating on a cloud in cannabis heaven.

I go back to bed.

After snoozing until ten, I get up and use some lady's fingernail polish remover to get rid of the blond goatee and re-dye my hair and eyebrows back to dark brown, then I hit the gym for a few quick reps and a shower and shave. It's good to be Mike Reardon again and not a blond dumpster diver, particularly if Speck and the Indians have any friends looking for the guy who smoked Speck in Rosie's parking lot.

I have mixed emotions about leaving my truck, camper and Wells Cargo trailer where they're parked, but knowing that Speck and the Indians were not on the best of terms with the Russians, wonder if I'm not a hero to Two Cents, Curly, and that bunch. I hope they're too busy with their upcoming meeting, and now with how they'll take over the Indian's territory, to worry much about me. But I'm sure that won't last long.

Just as I'm thinking of Two Cents, my phone buzzes. "Yeah," I answer in my normal polite manner.

"What the fuck, *pendajo*," Two Cents says, then laughs, "you let a little shoot-out keep you from doing our deal?"

I laugh quietly in return. "Didn't think you'd want me leading the cops your way."

"No shit." Then he sounds as little suspicious. "How'd you get out of the can so quick?"

"My second cousin's a bondsman over in Wyoming, he made a deal with some local guy…and I told them I took the gun I used away from one of the bad guys who was trying to rob us. They doubted it, but they bought it finally, cause I didn't waiver." I don't mention that I had a holster on my belt and nobody would be so stupid as to miss that, but he doesn't know it either, as all I said during our meeting in his Expedition was that I was carrying.

"How much bail?"

"Fifty gee's. Cost my cousin five grand. But he knows I'm good for it."

His voice seems a little suspicious. "So, *cuales tu pinche pedo*?"

"Hey, I don't speak that shit."

"What's your fucking problem? What'd they bust you for?"

It's time to get creative. "Hey, that fucking cop the dead broad was with had a hard on for me cause I walked out the same time she did. They put accessory to murder on the paperwork, but you know that's bullshit and so do they. They just wanted to twist me up to see what I know."

"So, *muchacha*, what the fuck did you tell them?"

"Hey, I know enough fucking Spanglish to know I ain't no *muchacha, muchacho*."

He laughs gruffly. "So, what. You spill your guts on our deal?"

"We didn't do no deal, and I don't talk shit to no cops no matter how hard they come down."

He's quiet for a moment, then asks, "You still got the two grand to make the deal?"

"Sure, when?"

"Can't do it on credit no more. You in the crosshairs of the man...too risky, *pendajo*. But you bring cash, you'll get the stash. I can give you a brick for two."

"I'll think about it."

"Don't think too long," he snarls, and disconnects.

It's time to play catch up, so I check my email and see that I do have a contract to pick up Speck, and have to laugh, as I farmed out the five grand Pax negotiated with the bondsman...but it was worth five grand to dust the son of a bitch.

I also get a fascinating report from Pax regarding the BP superintendent. There's nothing in his background, at least not so far, that would make us think he's a bad guy...then, oops, it seems he's a slumlord. He owns all three properties that are frequented by the bad boys. The section west of town, the doublewide out off 136th, and, I hope he's insured, the barn and eighty acres northeast of town that we just visited and burned to the ground. I no more than finish my email when my phone buzzes again with Pax's ring.

"Wha's up?" I answer.

"Not the temperature," he says. "It's cold as hell here, below freezing last night," he complains.

"You're breaking my friggin' heart. I'm in North Dakota and you're telling me you're cold?"

"Yeah, yeah, I know. Anyway, the computers up your way have been buzzing since midnight. You been busy?"

I relate to him the events of the last twelve hours.

"You been busy," he concurs, then adds, "you know about this big meeting late today?"

"You get a time from any of your Trojan Horse work?"

"Best we can figure it's set for six o'clock. It's a peace treaty and reorganization, since a good part of the Indian contingency is out of the picture. The Russians are even bringing the pizza and beer." That gives me an idea, but I let him go on.

"And?" I ask.

"And it's in the 'building next to the plant,' is the best I can get.

"There're two Quonset huts out west of town, you know the spot. One of them is a meth lab, and I presume 'the plant' in question. The meeting must be in the other. Text or call me when you know the Expedition is heading that way."

"You got it."

Just after noon I head for DiAngelo's and a sausage sandwich, or maybe a bowl of that good tripe soup.

It's time to be well fed as it could be another long night. I have to presume this meeting is out of town in the Quonset hut, but it could be in the doublewide out off 136th, or anywhere else. I hope it's not the doublewide as it appeared to be housing for the stable of girls, and the Quonset a lab for the manufacture of meth. I don't want to have to worry about a bunch of poor Russian girls, who probably thought they were coming to America to become famous fashion models, getting caught up in the crossfire.

The place is packed and I have to wait, even for a seat at the bar, and am just finishing my sandwich about one thirty when Tony comes in. I catch his glance, and note that he's sporting a couple of bandages on his cheeks and a couple on his neck, but other than that again looks like he just stepped out of GQ magazine.

He ignores me and finds a table against the wall. In seconds his table is surrounded by townspeople offering their condolences and trying to get the story about what happened.

I see a copy of the local paper left on the bar and ask the bartender to bring it over, but I guess the incident out at the barn was too late to make the news, then glance up at a TV over the bar and see the camera panning the burned out barn. I can't hear the audio, so I grab my phone and find an app for the local TV station, and read about the ongoing investigation into what's being described as a dope dealer war.

I don't smile, but want to.

Chapter Twenty Five

As I'm reading, my phone buzzes and I have to abandon the story to answer. "Ola," I say, knowing from caller ID that it's Pax.

He doesn't bother with a greeting. "I can't get crap on this Nickleston guy other than the property ownership thing. But I know deep in my black little heart that there's more to this asshole. Get me some fingerprints."

"I'll make that happen. Anything else new?"

"Yeah, I saw Jennifer last night."

"Cool, I'm sure she asked about me, pining for my return."

"Actually she was with some cat who's a pit boss where she works...all cuddled up and trading spit. She referred to you as a will-o-the-wisp."

I'm a little disappointed as I had high hopes for the girl.

"I guess that's better than a limber dick." I at least get a laugh out of Pax. "There were no promises made nor commitments," I continue, with some nonchalance I don't really feel. But I'll get over it.

"She looked a little embarrassed when she saw me, but I walked right up and stuck my hand out to the guy. He seemed like a decent dude."

"Good for her." I decide to change the subject. "Nothing else business wise?"

"Yeah, you got an email from some dot com cat in Santa Barbara who's missing a G5 and the SBPD and the FBI and the CIA and the DEA and the FAA and CBS, NBC, ABC and every other acronym are stumped. I guess he worked his way down to the SOB at the bottom of the barrel."

"Yeah, FU you DS. Let's see, a fifty million dollar aircraft should be worth a tidy recovery fee."

"What's a DS?"

"Dipshit."

"The good news," Pax continues without a retort, "he said a mil, but I'm sure it's worth more to him."

"Insurance will cover it—"

"No theft insurance, just liability. This doofus has so much of the publics initial offering money paid cash for it, so no requirement I guess."

That makes me smile. "Sounds like at least three mil."

"I'll have a full file on him, the plane, and his employees and relatives down to third cousins when you get back. So get back here safe and ready to make me a pile of dough."

"From your lips to God's ears, brother. I should wind this up in a couple of days, with luck."

"Stay well, stay alive, get me some prints," he says, and rings off.

Since I'm already on the phone, I dial Tony DiAngelo, who's only across the room, but neither of us wants to be seen with the other.

"What's up," he answers.

"I'm off to visit a fun place this PM. You going, or is your...." I start to say blood-lust satisfied, but I am talking on a cell, so I refrain, "...yourself available, or do you want to pass?"

"Meet me out back. I'll go through the kitchen, you go out the front."

"Yes, sir," I say, and act like I'm still talking after he rings off.

My van is only two parking places from the front door, so I drive, and by the time I get around and into the alley, Tony is waiting by the dumpster.

He doesn't bother with a howdy. "I'm going, but I'm driving myself...time I started distancing myself from the very, very illegal side of this crap."

I have to chuckle. "Hell, seems like we were defending ourselves last night."

He shakes his head, seemingly a little astonished, "Yeah, blowing a retreating vehicle half way to the friggin' moon is definitely self-defense."

I shrug, and can't help but smile. "Well, there is that...," then I get serious, "you having second thoughts?"

"No, I'm not. I want Amber's soul to rest in peace, if at all possible...just not while I'm doing twenty five to life in a place where ex-cops have to be in solitary for the duration. By the way, I registered you with the department as a confidential informant, so we have some reason to be talking back and forth."

I reach into the glove compartment and dig out a handheld radio. "That's fine, but still, better we don't use the cell phone. My tech guys have rigged these to a channel that's not on the normal scans, so we can talk freely. I've got some homework to do, then I'll call you on the cell. Subtract three hours from anytime I mention, and that's when I'll be here," I hand him a note with a map to the Quonset huts. "When you get within three or four miles, turn on your radio. Leave your cell phone in your desk, just in case anyone wants to track your whereabouts via it."

He nods.

So I continue. "Let's clean this place up." And I head out of the alley for the camper.

I've been remiss in not tagging this guy Nickleston's car with a tracking device, so I look up the offices of Bakken Production and head north on 136th, and am not surprised to find it's only about a mile past the turnoff to the doublewide trailer he owns and some of the scumbags occupy.

BP's office appears to be a remodeled school building; one that might have had half a dozen classrooms at one time. There's even a bell tower over the entry.

I drive around to the back of the building where a number of vehicles are parked. A dozen tan trucks, all crew cabs, most GMC's, and a few cars, both company vehicles and private ones. But there's only one crew cab tan truck with a camper shell on the back, and it's one of only four that appears brand new.

And there's a parking space right beside it, so I slide in even though I can see that the concrete bumper in front of the place has a name on it. I don't plan to be here long. I slide across into the passenger bucket seat of the van, and study Nickleston's truck for a moment.

From my elevated view in the van I can see there's a Coke can in the holder and a couple on the floor, so I step out, open his door, and gather up three Coke cans and a couple of cigarette butts out of the ashtray.

And then circle the van, climb back into the driver's seat, and start it up. As I'm backing out, some old boy with a puss gut runs out of the backdoor of the building, shouting at me.

I presume Nickleston's office faces the rear and he saw me burgling his car. As I slip the van in gear, he hits the end of the walkway and slips on the icy walk, tries to recover, then his feet go out from under him and he hits flat on his back, hard.

It's the first good laugh I've had since well before the humor went out of my life as I held Amber's head in my lap and stared into formerly beautiful blue eyes, now gone glassy.

He's trying to set up as I make the turn at the end of the building. It's childish, but I can't help but give him the finger as I disappear from view.

I drive straight to a pack and ship and get a strange look from the clerk when I buy an overnight FedEx box and stuff it with the garbage from Nickleston's truck, and spend almost fifty bucks to ship it overnight to Las Vegas. It's all I can do not to talk in tongues to the kid so he's absolutely convinced I'm a fruitcake, but instead I wish him a merry Christmas and head out.

It's time to check the Wells Cargo trailer out and see what I might need to make the world come to an end for a gaggle of scumbags.

Chapter Twenty Six

This time I might just have the opportunity to get in some sniper work. When you may be up against multiple enemies it's imperative you give yourself all the advantage you can, and distance, when guys are shooting short barreled weapons such as automatic pistols and short range weapons such as shotguns and most pistols, is an advantage. Particularly when you have a SASS, a semi-auto sniper system.

I was unable to find a Marine Corps model after having to deep six my last one, but the US Army XM110 Semi-Automatic Sniper Rifle with daylight telescope sight, night vision telescope sight, bipod, and quick-detachable sound suppressor. It's painted in desert camo, but where I plan to set up is amongst the fallen branches of a cottonwood, so it should be fine.

Trying to determine who might be at this surfeit of skunks, and deciding that it should be at the minimum a half dozen Russians—Bogdan the bear; Vasily aka V-1 and Vlad; Victor, aka V-2; Luthor with the missing ear lobe; and maybe other assholes I've yet to meet—and of course Alverado Cenzano, aka Big Al and Two Cents; and Guillermo Soto aka Tamale…I take six clips of .308's.

I've replaced the short barrel on both the Colt M4's and take them and another six sets of two thirty round clips taped together, the spare is in case I tie up with Tony and he wants to go the fully auto route again. I load my belt, my battle rattle, with three flash grenades and three concussion grenades, but doubt if I'll have use for them as crashing into a room is one thing, but crashing into a Quonset hut that's over a hundred feet long and probably open the whole way is another all together, particularly when it's full of armed a-holes. On one thigh I'll have a .40 cal Glock with three extra clips and on the other my combat knife…not that I can imagine getting close enough to use it. As this may be going into the jaws of hell, I also load my Kevlar body armor and MICH Level IIIA Advanced Combat Ballistic Helmet, it's also Kevlar.

Should my former Marine staff-sergeant be watching, I'm sure he'd be a little surprised to see me dig in a cabinet and retrieve a pretty little yellow and green teddy bear, and put it with my load of goodies.

I don't dress in all white, but load my snow gear in the van, and am ready as I'll ever be. Locking things back up I head for the driver's seat of the van and hear the doors on the bus next door open and close, and move around to see Curly's skank heading for a Subaru wagon, and give her a yell, just to satisfy my curiosity if nothing else, "Hey, beautiful, is Curly home?"

"Yeah, he's inside, suckin' on a beer as usual."

So I wave and walk over and beat on the doors, and he opens them and stands there in a rag of a robe, sweat socks, and Uggs, looking like a refugee from Bergen-Belsen Nazi concentration camp, with his long hair, sunken cheeks, and sallow complexion. "Wha's up?" he asks.

"I got a few errands to run, but them I'll be back here…about six…with some pizzas and a six-pack. You guys gonna be around."

"Shit ya," he says, and gives me a smile flashing yellow teeth.

"Cool," I say, and head for the van. The skank is standing by the Subaru, I guess curious why I'm coming to see Curly, and I hear him yell at her as I climb into the van, "Who the fuck was that," and laugh as I realize I'm sans the blond hair, beard, and mustache.

"Or neighbor…I think," she answers, as I fire up the van and head out.

Obviously Curly's not in the inner circle of scum bags if he's not invited to the meeting.

It's only mid-afternoon, and I'm sure as hell not hungry as I had a fat meatball sandwich and bowl of zuppa trippa, and ate it all only a couple of hours ago, but none-the-less I stop at Wildcat Pizza and order six of the mondo size; three meatatarian and three Hawaiian, and blow one hundred thirty five bucks, which is maybe a little more than enough for my supper—but I have a plan for them.

I stop in a alley near the edge of town, dig in the back of the van for my pizza coveralls, and pull them on over my Kevlar vest and Kevlar ice skater's leggings, then apply my magnetic red and green stripes to the white van and a Rollie's Pizza & Chicken sign, in stylish red and green, to each side of the truck. I leave my red and green hat, with a yellow plastic simulated chicken's beak for a brim in the passenger seat. The leggings I only use when I think I might be going into a hail of gunfire, but they do offer some protection. If you get a femoral artery blown out, it's about as final as center chest. Originally designed for ice skating speed racers to keep them from being cut up when they tangle with another racer and go down, the leggings serve my purpose almost as well.

There's no question a guy would have to be a fool to take on a dozen guys if he could avoid it, particularly when they're well trained and well armed. I have no idea what kind of training these guys might have had, but have no doubt they're well armed...not as well as I am, but even a dozen badly armed guys can get lucky.

Before I head out, I make a phone call to Tony DiAngelo and ask if he's coming to the party at nine p.m., three hours later than the actually starting time of the meeting. I hope he remembers to subtract three hours as I instructed. I can hear music and laughter in the background as we talk, and I presume he's at his pop's restaurant...and staying sober.

It's one of those gray days where the horizon disappears into the snow covered hills and it's almost impossible to tell where hills end and sky begins, but at least it's not snowing, which would preclude the use of a long distance weapon.

I'm in no hurry, so I dial up a little easy listening on the Sirius, and take it slow and easy on the icy roads. Again I get a little Katy Perry and her *Roar* talks about the eye of the tiger, and I decide it's time to get in that frame of mind.

The weather's holding when I reach the section of land with the Quonset huts in it's middle, and I decide to drive the perimeter, and do. The slight indentation of my tracks are still in the grove of box elders, and the snow is only a little deeper than it was the last time I was here, so I figure I can park there again, safely. I make the full circle, passing the gate and driveway to the Quonsets, and note that there's not another gate, other than a couple of barb wire pull gates, anywhere in the perimeter of the place. The swing gate at the driveway stands open, to my surprise. There are a number of vehicle tire tracks already leading into the place, and I note a black Hummer parked a couple of hundred yards up the driveway, off to the side, and it's running, obviously, judging from the exhaust billowing into the cold. The windows are so dark I can't make out how many guys are checking who comes to the party.

I make another circle, only this time stop out of sight of the Hummer, a quarter mile back from the gate, opposite the way cars might be coming from town, and wait. I have one more piece of biz before I roll up the driveway, and reach into the glove department and grab the walrus mustache I've stowed there and use the makeup glue and mirror to attach it. That, and the hat with the yellow chicken beak bill, and pair of wide rimmed black eyeglasses, and I look like a pure dork trying to make an extra buck fighting the snow and ice to deliver pizza fifteen miles out of town…what a way to make a living.

The sun soon disappears behind me, and I check my watch. It's fifteen to six, and dark, and I, for the fourth time, check my handheld radio to make sure it's turned on…and it is, and I still haven't heard from DiAngelo. Where the fuck is he?

In another fifteen minutes, I say fuck it to myself, and fire up the van, pull it into drive, and head for the gate. It's time to do a little serious close up recon, even if I have no backup.

Chapter Twenty Seven

I turn into the driveway and see that the Hummer is still parked at the edge of the lane, and still running. As I near, some no-neck in an oversize pair of ski bibs climbs out and walks to the center of the lane, carrying a combat shotgun. I wave like some dudly-dumb-shit and stop and roll the window down, and he waddles up to the front fender and yells at me.

"You lost," he asks, and I realize he has a bit of a lisp.

"Hell no," I say, "I been looking all over for this place. Two Quonset huts and a big party, right?"

He's one of those guys whose nose is half the width of his face, but turned up a little hog-like, and his brows are deep and low, shades of Neanderthal cave dwellers. He has a smoking cigarillo in the hand not holding the shotgun, with both hands in mittens. If he's not locked and loaded, he's easily taken, but then the passenger side Hummer door opens and some equally ugly, this time cocoa brown cat—I think Samoan defensive tackle—holding another combat shotgun, stares at me through the crack between door and windshield, and rests the barrel of the shotgun there.

I've got to talk my way past these assholes. Luckily, the pizzas are on the passenger seat. I reach over and open a box and take half a Hawaiian and fold it in half and hand it out the window. "I bet you guys are ready for a slice?" I ask with a stupid grin.

The Neanderthal turns to the guy in the truck and yells, "Did Two Cents or Luther say anything about a pizza guy?"

I watch carefully as the guy in the truck sits his shotgun aside and dismounts, as he rounds the door, he yells back, "No, but he said there'd be pizza and beer, and I didn't see no pizza ovens in there. I want half of that, you fucker."

The Neanderthal puts the cigar in his mouth and reaches over and takes the half pizza out of my hand as I continue the stupid grin, and idle the van away. As I do so, I hear a yell behind me, but it's not "stop," it's "hey, where's the fucking beer." I ignore him, and roll on. Topping a rise a hundred yards beyond the Hummer, I see the Quonset huts in the distance, and surrounding them in front are a dozen vehicles, and as I get closer I see that one of them is a black Ford Expedition.

These guys are pretty serious about security, as I get close enough for my headlights to sweep the front of the huts, I see another guy is outside the door, standing slapping his hands together, and holding a machine pistol, an Uzi maybe.

I stop I reach over and run a finger inside a small tear in the back of teddy, and flip a switch on the battery powered microphone located there.

I double park behind a row of cars and trucks facing in toward the huts, and climb out carrying the pizza boxes.

"What the fuck," the guy at the door says, but he doesn't raise his Uzi to cut down a guy in a hat that makes him look like Charley the Chicken.

I yell with confidence I don't quite feel. "Pizza man, catch the door will you?"

This guy doesn't look like he's gotten his doctoral degree from Harvard, but he does mind well. He's looking a little confused, but opens the door for me and I sweep inside to see a forty foot wide Quonset hut, with some bunk beds, a heater made from a fifty gallon drum on edge, a cord of split wood stacked behind, a couple of rooms eighty feet away which are probably a kitchen and a shower room and bath, and at least eighteen guys, and I'm sorry to say, six women—and even sorrier to note that I know one of them.

The colorful Vanna White, still with canary yellow legs.

The girls are all lined up perpendicular to the head table, and don't look happy. In fact, no one does.

There's a couple of folding tables like you'd find in a school cafeteria, one of which supports a pony keg of beer in a half barrel lined with ice, and a dozen medium size pizza boxes...the tightwads. There are at least two dozen folding chairs with their backs to me, facing another folding table where four guys are plopped on folding chairs. I can see that one of them is Two Cents, one is the stubby eared Luthor, and two of the Russians, the Bear and one of the V boys.

A guy I've never seen hustles over and, not kindly, puts a hand in the middle of my chest before I reach the pizza table.

"Hey, we got our pizza, motherfucker. What's this?"

"Don't know, sir. It's paid for." He eases up, except for the deeply furrowed brows, and I plop the boxes on the table among the others, and hand him the bear.

"Free teddy bear with every four large pizzas."

"Get the fuck out of here," he says, and gives me a push.

I stop a little out of his reach and look heartbroken. "Give the bear to one of your kids." Then look even more crestfallen. "Fifteen miles, and no tip?"

"Get the fuck—" he starts to say, but I spin on my heel and head for the door, and it's a good thing I do as my walrus mustache is half falling off. I pat it back into place as I head out the door and pass the guard.

Over my shoulder I snap at the guy, "Great pizza and those fucking tightwads got no tip for me."

He yells after me. "I got a tip for you, get the fuck out of here."

I wave over my shoulder, fire up the van, pass the Hummer at about twenty miles an hour, sliding from side to side, blowing snow and mud out behind the van, and am soon on the country lane and out of sight. While inside I noted a gun rack on both sides of the hut, long arms, military style. I didn't want to stare, so only glanced, but there were at least two dozen, some I recognized as AK47's, and most of them with banana clips.

I turned the handheld radio off before I approached the Hummer in the first instance, and now turn it back on and push the send, "Tony, where the hell are you?"

But there's no answer. I drive the perimeter of the section and park in the grove of box elders, ditch the pizza coveralls in the back and trade them for a white snow gear, load up a back pack with water, my radio, ammo, and strap on my binocs with their hug-the-chest strap, my battle rattle belt, thigh holster and scabbard, then grab my combat helmet—it's black, which is okay in the darkness—with it's tiny LED headlamp, attach it's night vision scope and sling the .308 over one shoulder and carry the M4 but don't bother to turn on the muzzle mounted combat light. The headlamp is enough, even though it's dark as hell as the moon is not yet up. In a few seconds I'm at the broken down section of the barbwire fence, and striding toward the out-of-place cottonwood on the crest of the hill, where I have a five hundred yard clear field of fire.

But it looks like this recon is for intel only, as I'm not about to start a war with a couple of dozen guys, particularly guys armed with Uzi's, AK's, and God only knows what else.

It's a good half hour to my planned emplacement, but it's as good as I remember. I clear a foot of snow off a fallen foot and a half diameter cottonwood, stomp the snow down behind it and arrange my gear so I have easy access, and in a few minutes I hope I'm a one man army, even though I'd planned to have someone flanking these bad guys, and equally well armed. But I guess that's not to be.

My last piece of business is to tune my handheld to the channel matching that of the transmitter and delicate microphone in the teddy bear, engage the recording app on my iPhone and set it next to the radio, and set back to listen and record the events of the evening. While I'm doing so, I focus the night vision binocs and then the scope on the SASS to the general distance of the buildings.

The first words I hear are a little distant and muted, but I swear the voice says, "kill them one at a time until they talk."

I have a pair of ear buds in my pack and dig them out and plug them into the radio, which kills the speaker and consequently the ability to record, but I have to be able to hear.

It seems there's a loud murmur and I can't make anything out, then a gunshot heard over the radio about blows my eardrums out.

I whip the ear buds off and rub my ears, then refit them to hear a guy screaming, "Get the fucking bitches outside. OUTSIDE! You're shooting holes in the fucking walls and if a stray one hits the wrong thing in the lab, we'll all be ground meat. And drag that fucking body out of here."

I hunker down and glue the binocs to my eyes. Even close up it's hard to know exactly what you're viewing through night vision equipment, and as figures begin to appear, walking to my side of the outside of the huts, I can't tell if they're men, or women, or even armed, but I can tell there's more than a dozen human beings.

Then I see one small figure sandwiched between two larger ones, it's arms seemingly over the shoulders of those flanking, and they fling it aside and it crumples into a snow bank and is still.

The body the guy wanted taken outside.

It's too damn cold to take a rest in the snow.

Then to my surprise, five more of the figures are lined up, then are forced down to their knees with large hands on much smaller shoulders.

I get a very cold feeling up my spine, even colder than the weather dictates, as I can't believe I'm seeing what I think is about to happen.

Grabbing up the SASS I bring it among the dozen figures, and just as I see one stride to the rear of those kneeling, flame leaps from a handgun he's holding, one of the kneeling figures pitches forward, and the roar of the shot snaps through the branches of the cottonwood under which I'm positioned.

The game...the rules of engagement, have changed.

Chapter Twenty Eight

I'd decided I wasn't about to engage two dozen well armed guys, but they left me no choice.

I'm probably fucked, but not before I fuck up a few of them. Mama didn't teach me to mistreat women, much less allow some one else to do so, and much much less allow someone to kill them.

I center the crosshairs on the shooter, take a breath, hold it, and squeeze. The SASS bucks in my cradle, and the guy is blown back, and others all turn facing my way. The suppressor makes the SASS almost impossible to hear at two hundred yards, much less five hundred, so they have no idea where the shot came from.

Those who'd been on their knees are up, and running away from the huts, into the snowfields, as I pan the crosshairs over the rest of them. I don't know who's a target, and who might be another poor Russian girl who thought she was headed for the fashion runway in Chicago or New York. Then I see fire spit from another weapon, bring the crosshairs to the middle of his mass, and pull off another, and he spins away and goes down, then the rest of the figures all break back toward the buildings, as screams and shouts echo across the snow, and the crowd is quickly out of sight.

I consider hauling ass for the van, but twenty minutes to get there would be the best I could do, and if these guys have half a brain, some of them will be in vehicles and soon circling the section. They could have a dozen guys in a half dozen trucks hunting for me, and they'll find the van long before I can reach it.

Deciding my best bet is to hunker down and see if they're stupid enough to stomp across the snowfields coming after an entrenched shooter who's already proven his marksmanship. I hope so.

Even with the suppressor on the SASS, a carful observer can spot the muzzle flash.

They are offering no targets, but I have one advantage, I can hear some of what's going down inside the non-lab hut, but the excited shouting is occluding most of it, but making some of it easier. And I hear the word, "Cops," and hope they think it's half the swat teams in North Dakota.

But I know that won't last for long, and it doesn't, as I hear "trucks," and focus on the vehicles parked in front. I'm still at a distinct disadvantage as I don't know who to target, then decide that it'll do no harm to bust up some trucks, and empty my first clip at the engine compartments of the trucks, but don't do much good as two of them fire up and head out, just about the same time as I realize my hidey hole has been spotted, as a half dozen weapons open up and the cottonwood tree overhead and the branch in front of me starts getting trimmed by what sounds to me like a cadre of AK's being fired.

Needless to say, I hunker lower in my hole and try to keep score. There were at least two dozen folks inside the hut, two of them are dead in the snow, probably women, at least five have hauled ass into the snowfields, again, probably Russian girls. I knocked the hell out of two. So if there were two dozen, now there are fifteen, and at least two, and probably four, have left in two trucks...not that I think I've seen the last of them. I'm sure they're on the hunt, they're the foxes, and I'm the rabbit.

As soon as the gunfire slows, then stops, I slip out the back of my hole and, on my belly in the eighteen inch deep snow, do the belly crawl thirty yards to the side—not easy in battle rattle and carrying two weapons—and staying as low as I can, beat down another makeshift hidey hole, and set up again with the bipod and SASS.

Now, it's be patient.

I don't have to be patient for long, as gunfire again opens up on my former location. I have a half dozen half decent targets of guys leaning around the sides of the Quonset huts, and firing from the two windows in back of the hut where the meeting was taking place, but I don't want to give away my location unless I have a sure kill.

The fire, as I suspected, is covering fire, and some is spitting chunks out of the log I used for cover. Some is kicking up snow many yards on both sides of their target, so some of them seem to be marksmen, some hacks. I hope the hacks aren't so bad I get killed by a guy trying to hit a target ninety feet from me.

But I fear I've under estimated some of these guys, for it's damn good shooting with an AK at five hundred yards to be consistently knocking chunks out of my log. At least some of these guys have had some time on the range with a good instructor.

I watch carefully through the binocs as they have a wider field of view than the scope, and sure as hell, two guys hustle off into the snow to the right, and another two to the left.

A little gift from God. I know the terrain well enough to know there's no real cover between them and the cottonwood. A few others are continuing their cover fire, so I get a wild idea and decide to give them some encouragement, and dislodge a flash grenade and lob it back to my former location, then turn the other way and cover my ears.

The blast lights up the night, and the noise is a shock wave across the snow.

The firing stops as they're trying to figure out if I've fired a cannon at them, or if something in my hole has blown up and scattered my meat all over the hillside.

I stay very quiet, and very still, wanting them to believe the latter.

The firing stops altogether, and I ease up over the edge of my new stomped hole, and sweep the binocs from side to side, picking out the two groups plugging through the snow, making their way up the hill.

My ear buds are worth listening to again, and I hear them discussing the possibility that I'm dead meat.

Keep coming boys, in fact send a couple more just for good measure. There are four on the hill, coming my way, and probably eleven back in the hut, or huts.

I let the boys headed up the hill cover two hundred and fifty of the five hundred, just so they can't get back home too quickly, then set up on the two the furthest away, the breeze is up, not that anything but a wind would matter too much at three hundred twenty six yards, which the rangefinder in my scope says is the target, but I compensate about three inches, and knock the guy in the lead ass end over teakettle, then pan to the guy following, who's now hauling ass at as hard a run as he can manage in the snow back to the huts. I lead him three feet, and squeeze off, and he, too, spins, throws his weapon end over end as he does, and hits the ground, but almost bounces back to his feet, and only slightly slower, keeps moving. The third shot of the series knocks him flying and he's down for the count.

Then all hell breaks loose all around me. I don't have the protection of the fat cottonwood log, and even as low as I can press myself into the snow, I can feel a slug crease my upper back, and one whacks my helmet so hard I'm seeing stars, and think, for a fleeting moment, that I've bought the farm.

But I shake off the rattling of my brain around inside my skull, and realize I still have two targets coming my way, and when I reposition the weapon on the edge of my hole, realize that I must have been out cold for a few moments. They're only fifty yards down the hill, and closing fast. I leave the SASS with the muzzle pointing up at a forty five degree angle, and grab the M4, and hunker even lower in the hole until I figure they're only twenty five yards and closing. Setting her to full auto, I drape my self over the edge of the hole and pan a burst of thirty .223's sweeping both runners, who are as quickly doing backward somersaults down the hill, then I pick up my weapons and run like a wild man at a diagonal down hill, until I realize I'm in a slight depression, and hit the snow again, as a hundred bullets cut the air overhead.

Chapter Twenty Nine

My back is burning like hell, and I hope it's nothing but a flesh wound, and not bleeding too badly, then I realize that I've taken one across the thigh. My head is aching and throbbing and I'm having a little trouble focusing, and am wondering if I don't have a concussion.

But even if I do, I have to stay awake, and alert. These guys are not the usual dipshit handgun-turned-sideways gangbangers. I'm wondering if these Russian guys weren't some of those in Afghanistan long before I was in Iraq.

They shoot like it's not their first rodeo.

I sigh deeply and wonder what the hell I'm doing here in a snow bank fighting half the Red Army for a lousy hundred grand when I could be in some tropical isle among bikini clad beauties hunting a beautiful G5 and looking to make three mil.

I hope my old CO forgets to call me next time…if there is a next time, and right now, I doubt it.

Fuck, I'm dizzy. I wonder if they'll find me if I just curl up, pull some snow over me, and go to sleep.

Then I hear the crackle of a radio, and someone speaking a foreign language, and the answer, in little more than a whisper, and it's "Da." Yes, in Russian, and the sound is not more than five or six yards down the hill from me.

I dislodge a concussion grenade from my battle rattle, pull the pin, give it a long three count, and barely lob it down hill, then hunker down shoving the helmet up as tightly against my ears as I can.

"WHAM," it goes off, and I pop up to see a guy stumbling downhill, not twenty feet away. I stitch him up the backbone with the M4, then stumble a few yards on downhill at a forty five degree angle from the huts, which are still over four hundred yards away. I'm hoping the crowd below won't fire as their man is in the neighborhood.

I find another depression, and fall into it.

It's all I can do not to close my eyes and go to sleep, but if I do, I know I won't wake up. I lay there for a few minutes, then decide I've got to take it to them if I want to live, and I think I know exactly how to do so.

Stumbling to my feet, I run straight for the nearest hut, and probably get a hundred yards before I begin to see muzzle flashes coming from the edges of the huts, and dive into a snow bank, and stay still as the snow around me kicks up and the air above me buzzes with bullets.

I dig my iPhone from a coat pocket to check the time, and see it's seven twenty, and that I've had a call from DiAngelo, but the last thing I want to do now is return a call, then I realize that I've left the radio set on a channel to pick up the mike in the teddy bear, and grab it out of my other coat pocket and switch it back to Tony's channel, and am returning it to my pocket when it buzzes and I put it to my hear and poke the send.

"Where the fuck have you been," I ask, in not too friendly a tone.

"I just got here. I thought you said nine o'clock?"

"I said three hours before the time I tell you."

"Sounds like a friggin' war up there. I'm at the gates and there's no one here—"

"There was a Hummer and two bad guys parked a couple of hundred yards up the driveway."

"Not here now."

"Okay, but don't come this way. Get off the driveway, and kill anything that comes that way. Be careful, I think there's five or six Russian girls stumbling around in the snow, trying to get the hell away from these guys."

"You got it. You're not coming this way?"

"Not until after I call you off. I'm going to try and light up the night again, if I can pull it off."

"Good luck, sorry I was late."

I merely grunt, then again break toward to huts. I want to be only a couple of hundred yards from them when I go to work on the lab. But I'm getting close enough that even a jerk who's a lousy shot might put me toes up, and with the first muzzle flash, I dive into the snow, and wait without moving.

I wait a good ten minutes. Then I eject the clip I've been using, put in a fresh one, lay the other one nearby, raise up, and start stitching the lab building from one end to the other. Snow is starting to bounce all around me as AK's light up the shadows. I pop the clip, reverse it, and stitch away, when something tears at my side and spins me to my back. But this is my only chance, I figure, and I insert my last clip…if this doesn't work, I'm using my Glock against a half dozen or more AK47's and I know where that'll end. I don't have time to worry about how many holes are poked in my already well-scarred bod.

So, I'm back up, and firing, then suddenly I'm slammed flat on my back, and if it wasn't for the brilliant light, I'd think I was already in the coffin. I hear things begin to fall back to earth, and raise up enough to see flames shooting forty feet above the former, now missing, ridge line of the hut, and across what's left of it to the meeting hut, which is blown all to hell as well, and pieces of corrugated tin are still floating, like deadly scimitars, out of the dark sky.

Fuck it, I'm going to sleep, and I lay back and cuddle down into the snow. If any of those assholes have lived through that, they can have me.

I lay back, then the chatter of gunfire over the low hill toward the gate disturbs my hoped for snooze, and I know it has to be DiAngelo trying to take on automatic weapons with his sidearm and possibly a combat shotgun.

There is no rest for the wicked. I'm on my feet and stumbling through the snow, then avoiding the parking lot where three vehicles are on fire, thanks, I imagine to the blast from the meth lab.

It's not often a mangled body makes one smile, but the one I pass in the parking lot has a stub of an ear on the three quarters of a head left on a mangled neck, and the stub doesn't look fresh like an explosion blew it away. I tromp on, until I can see the crest of the hill, and two guys hiding behind a black Expedition. I find a stock watering trough, and hunker down behind it, maybe a hundred and fifty yards from the Ford, and get back on my radio.

"You listening?" I ask.

It's a moment, and I have to pay attention as the two guys behind the black Ford are firing toward the gate, hiding using the Ford for cover.

It's a five count, but then Tony is on. "Yeah, I'm at the gate, using my vehicle for cover. You okay?"

"A little shot to shit, but still ticking. You want to see another fireworks show?"

"You don't mean…?"

"Stay down."

"You got it," he says.

I dial a number on my iPhone, and when it answers punch in my birthday, plus a day, count to three, then the world lights up again as the heavy Ford does a full flip and lands back on it's wheels, but the tires have been blown away, and it's burning like hell. The two gunmen are out of sight, needless to say, and probably fodder for the coyotes. I'm sure an environmental report would not condone my feeding the coyotes spoiled Russian chunks.

"Nice one," comes from my phone.

"Thank the US Marine Corps demolition training course," I say, then add, "any chance you can pick me up about fifty feet on the other side of that burning vehicle?"

"It would be my pleasure."

I stumble around the Ford, keeping some distance as I don't know if the gas tank's blown yet, but can't imagine it hasn't, and by the time I get twenty yards past it and rejoin the driveway, Tony's waiting.

"We got to get out of here," I mumble as I climb into the passenger seat, "before the cops come."

"I am the cops."

"I mean the pussy cops, who don't believe in real justice."

"Right. You want to go to the hospital, I presume. You look like a hog that's half butchered."

"Unless you know someone else who can patch me up. But this will be hard to explain to a hospital staff. I've got a side wound which may have broken a rib, maybe a concussion 'cause I'm seeing two of you and believe me one is ugly enough, a crease, or maybe worse, across the back, and a one across my thigh...and who knows until I get stripped down."

"My sister's a nurse. If I ask, she'll put you up until you heal up, and you couldn't get better care. But you've got to keep your hands to yourself. Go to sleep, it's a little bit of a ride."

"Cool," I manage to mumble. "I like Italian cooking," and I doze off.

Chapter Thirty

I'm laying in a frilly bedroom, all pink and lacy, wondering how long it's been since I've slept in a bed under a down comforter, when I hear a low knock on the door.

"Yes," I manage, and the door opens a couple of inches and a dark eye with long lashes is peeping at me, then the door opens wider and a very good looking woman stands smiling at me.

"I was beginning to worry that you'd never awaken," she says, then asks, "coffee, tea?" and even in my debilitated state I'm hoping she'll add, "or me?" but it's wishful thinking.

But she does add, "I'm Tony…Antonia to my family, but Tony Two to my friends. Sometimes my family just calls me Tu, or Tu Tu…it gets a little confusing. Why parents would name kids Anthony and Antonia has always been beyond me…."

"Coffee would be great," I say, with as much smile as I can muster, and she disappears. My head is hurting like hell, I'm laying on what is obviously stitches, by the pokes, in my back. I run a hand down my thigh, and feel stitches there, but it's my side that hurts the worst, with every breath. It's not my first busted rib, but my first bullet-busted rib.

In moments she's back with a tray with a carafe of coffee and some buttered raisin toast, with a small bowl of sugar and a little pitcher of cream.

"I forgot to ask how you take it," she says, as she pours.

Pushing myself up to a sitting position, I don't manage without a grimace. I have to clamp my jaw to keep from moaning.

"Hurts?" she asks.

"Yeah, a little…but I've hurt worse."

She laughs, a nice tinkle, and says, "Yeah, I saw that you've had some rough times. If you had a buck for every stitch scar on that hard body of yours you'd be a rich man."

That makes me wonder about the fee I hope to have coming, but it's a passing thought as getting well is the first thing on the agenda.

I manage a smile. "Seems like I've got a few more, here and there. Is that your good work?"

"My brother, Tony One, doesn't ask me for much, but he asked me to take care of you…to watch out for you, in more ways than one," and she winks at me with those long lashes, "but to get you well. He'll be back this afternoon."

"Where am I, exactly?" I ask.

"You, sir, are in beautiful downtown Ray, North Dakota, thirty some miles north east of Williston. My husband, Alex, is pastor of the Lutheran Church here, and it's just next door."

Now I'm embarrassed about what I was thinking.

"Did my phone get here?"

"It did. It's on the dresser with your wallet and the first firearm that's ever been in this house other than the one my brother wears. There's a bathroom through that door, not fancy, but not bad for rectory housing."

I start to take a bite of the toast, but she takes my other hand and I pause, then she bows her head, "Thank you father for this sustenance we're about to receive. God bless us, this house, and make this fine man whole again. Amen."

Now I'm really feeling bad for what I was thinking.

"Amen," I add. "Just black on the coffee, please," and she pours, smiles, and heads for the door.

"I'll have a real breakfast for you. You want it in bed?"

"No, ma'am. In about an hour, if that's okay. If you'll hand me my phone I've got a call to make, then I'm going to get in the shower, or at least take a spit bath."

"You can shower. I've got good dressings on you and can redo them. An hour would be good as I have to head over to the old folks home and make my nursing rounds...you sure you don't need help getting in the shower?"

Again, I have to quell my thoughts, and then redden a little. "No, ma'am, I'm a big boy."

"Yeah," she says, pulling the door shut, "I noticed," and she giggles as she heads down the hallway.

Pax answers on the first ring. "I've followed your escapades on the Williston news. They didn't mention finding your ugly carcass so I figured you crawled away."

"Thanks for worrying. I've got a little heal up time, then I think I'm done here, and hope so, a little time by the pool in the warm sun would be welcome."

"Bullshit, you've got a plane to catch, a G5...and I mean snare, not catch in the airport sense."

"Right, after I heal up."

"So, what do you need?"

"Someone to drive the van back while I drive the truck and camper."

"Skip is back from Europe, broke, and ready to go back to work."

"He blew a cool mil already. That boy must have had some kind of good time. Send him up in say, three days. I'll be gimpy, but well enough to drive, presuming my head heals."

"How many holes you got in you...and tell me what went down."

I spend twenty minutes playing catch up with him, and twenty minutes sitting in the bottom of the shower letting the hot water cook the edge off the aches and pains in the old bod. The most interesting thing he has for me is the result of the fingerprints that he recovered from the Coke cans I sent him that I recovered from Nickleston's truck. He does not have any wants and warrants, but he does have a record. He was fired twenty years ago for taking bribes while working as the superintendent in a California oilfield, and arrested, but got off on a three year probation...and he's changed his name since then. Morris Alberton became Morris Nickleston, and I'll bet he's got a total phony new background in order to get the good job he now holds.

Only then do I manage to get to Tu's table for a plate full of scrambled eggs, Italian sausage, fresh fruit, and some kind of twisted bread filled with dried fruit. If my side didn't hurt every time I chewed or breathed, I'd be in hog-heaven…still, it ain't bad duty.

There's a small sunroom-greenhouse off the kitchen, and a chaise lounge, and I ask if it's okay to crash there, and in a few moments am sleeping off the great breakfast while Tu is tending to the old folks and I presume her husband to the flock.

Alex, Tu's husband and the pastor, is a fine man, as one would imagine, with short gray hair and a close-cropped beard over his white Lutheran pastor's collar. He does seem to think I need some serious work in the soul-saving department, and I pray with him daily, penance for my recent sins which he seems to have some knowledge of. We do enjoy several games of cribbage while I heal.

I'm totally pampered for three days, until Skip, another old Marine buddy and bounty hunting sidekick, calls me on the cell from the Williston airport.

Neither of my hosts are there when Skip shows up in a rental car, so I find an envelope and leave a thank you note along with five crisp Franklins, a cell phone number and an email address, and head out.

It seems my van has not been discovered by the plethora of cops who combed the desolated Quonset hut site, but it also appears some of the bad guys found it, so it was a good thing I didn't try to beat feet back there when the bullets started to fly. I guess they didn't want me to sneak in it and drive away while they were hunting for me, as all four tires have been slashed.

I call Triple A for a tow, explain the situation, and they send a rig out and we manage to winch it up on the back of one of those tilt bed trucks. I have to transfer a few select items from the van to Skip's rental car.

Then we head for my truck, camper, and Wells Cargo trailer, and I'm pleased to find it all still in place.

I turn to skip and say, "Back me up," and he nods as I head next door to the bus and rap on the door.

The skank answers, sees who it is, and opens the folding doors.

"Curly?" I ask and she waves us in.

Even though I'm still gimping, Skip, who's a Viking blond type with a barrel chest that is imposing even without the eighteen inch arms, is close behind.

Curly, as usual, is laying on his ass, in a ragged robe, watching some soap on the tube.

"Curly, pay close fucking attention," I say, and he looks up and shrugs.

"You shrug one more time, or even blink, and we'll burn this piece of shit bus down around your ugly ears."

That gets his undivided attention, and he slips a hand down into the crack between the cushions on the beat up couch, but only gets it halfway in, when both Skip and I have weapons pulled and centered on his chest.

"What the fuck…?" he mumbles, but pulls the hand back and folds both of them in his lap.

"I'm sure you're thinking that you can step up to big time in the dope arena, now that most your buddies are coyote bait—"

"That was you?" he stutters.

"You don't need to know anything but the route out of North Dakota. I've got a couple of errands to run, and if this bus is here when I get back, you'll be a sorry miserable piece of dog shit…you got it."

He nods, hard enough to dislocate his neck.

I continue. "And I don't mean just out of Williston, I mean out of the state. I'm surprised the PD or state police haven't picked you up already as I gave them your name on a list."

"I'm gone man," he says. "Arizona, or someplace warm."

Skip and I fade out the door, but watch him as we go. I hear the skank yell "motherfucker," and him snap, "shut the fuck up and tie shit down." Now I've got one more call to make before I haul ass out of North Dakota.

It's time to run a high placed executive out of the state, close behind Curly.

Chapter Thirty One

This time, even as gimpy as I am, I don't need Skip and ask him to remain in the waiting room of BP Production.

When I ask for Nickleston, the girl walks away from her reception desk for a minute or so, then returns. "Sorry, Mr. Reardon, you don't have an appointment. He's got meetings all day."

"Okay, but I want you to do me a big favor."

"And that is?" the very officious receptionist asks, as she takes her seat.

"Try one more time for me, only tell him this time that it's Mr. Appleton."

"I can't do that, he's busy."

I lean forward, resting both hands, knuckles down, on her desktop, and this time I give her my most ominous glare. "Young lady, I don't much give a damn if he's busy. You tell him Mr. Appleton is here and wants to see him." Then I flash the bail enforcement officer's badge at her.

She almost trips trying get out of the reception room and down the hall, and this time is back in fifteen seconds.

"He says he'll see you in the conference room, but I'm to call security."

"You can call the KGB, FBI, and CIA for all I give a rat's ass. Where's the conference room?"

Skip remains in his seat, a cat-ate-the-canary grin on his face.

Nickleston is standing behind a conference table that would seat two dozen when I stride into the room. The girl, from behind me, asks, "Mr. Nickleston, should I call the police too?"

"Not yet," he says, giving me a gruff look, then asks, "So, is it Appleton or Reardon."

"I'm Reardon, and you're Appleton, and here's the way it's going to be—"

"What are you talking about?" he says, but his face is flushing.

"First, turn off any recording device you have working this room…and I know you do."

"There's nothing—"

"You dumb fuck, you don't want what I'm going to say recorded."

He moves to the end of the table, reaches under it, and I can hear a switch flip.

"Now, asswipe," I say, with all the growl I can muster, "you know fucking well what I'm talking about."

He turns from flushed red to pale white. "You're the asshole who cleaned out my truck the other day."

"Yeah, when you fell on your fat ass and I flipped you off. And yes, I got your prints off the cans, and, yes, I know you were Appleton until you lied to BP and used false ID and probably false credentials to get a job, and I'll bet if I look on your office wall, I'll find phony diplomas and God knows what else."

He actually backs away a step, until his back is both literally and figuratively against the wall. "I've had this job for ten years. Not this job, but a job with BP...for ten years. What do you want? Is this blackmail?"

"No. You're turning in your resignation. You're leaving the state, and the industry. I'm sending everything I know about you to the corporate headquarters of your mother company and the Investment bank that did their last underwriting, and I hope you get fucked out of any retirement you've built up, and I'm sending the same to every insurance company in the country. If I were you I wouldn't try to find another job other than flipping burgers."

"Why are you doing this?" he stammers.

"Because you're part of the problem and you've been working with the dope dealers...how, I don't know exactly, but I know you have. If you want me to keep investigating, I'll get enough on you to turn your dumb crooked ass into both the state and local cops, and maybe they'll put your ass away for a couple of dozen years." I start moving toward the door and stop before exiting and turn back. "I hate fucking dope dealers, and if they don't put you in a hole deep in the graystone mansion, then I'll come back and put you deep in a hole out in the oilfields where you'll never be found. If you watch the news, you know I'm just the boy to do it. You have a clear understanding of what I'm saying."

"Ye..ye...yes," he stammers.

"I'm checking back here in a week, and you fucking well better be gone."

I hear him say, "I will...I will," as I head down the hall.

As we head back into town, I make another phone call, on a throwaway, and the Colonel picks right up.

"You were a busy boy last night. I wondered if I'd ever hear from you again, or maybe they'd find your DNA in that bloody mess you left. Shades of Fallujah."

"Tough luck, Colonel," I say with a chuckle, "I'm still around. Is this a cash and carry deal."

"If you're happy with your work, it is."

"I'm happy."

"Swing by the office, there's a briefcase here with your name on it."

Now, for a week or so by the pool in Vegas, letting the sun heal me up, then, with any luck, and if Pax has the contract he went after, I'm off to hunt the illusive fifty million dollar G5.

Here's a look at the next Mike Reardon, The Repairman novel:

G5, Gee Whiz

by

L. J. Martin

Chapter One

Peace, at last, by the pool in Vegas, with a beautiful woman by my side...but peace has never been on top my priority list, and it doesn't take long until the urge to kick-ass kicks into gear. It seems to be an inverse reaction in my psyche, when my pain decreases and wounds heal, my aggression and craving for adrenaline increases. I know, I know, it's a personality flaw...or so the women in my life have oft told me, usually with great disdain, but occasionally, thank God, with increased interest.

Prather K. Wedgewood, or I should say one of his secretaries, called at least sixteen times during the two weeks it took me to heal up from my last repairman job, in Williston, North Dakota where I was helping out—for a substantial fee—my old CO from my Marine Recon unit in Iraq. The dope trade was costing his company at least a mil a year in accidents, insurance premium increases, and down time so I flushed some of the scum down the drain, but it cost me a concussion from a 150 grain across my battle helmet, a deep crease across my back, one gouge across a thigh, and a punch in and out of my side that clipped a rib but thank God not a bowel...all from AK47's badly aimed, I'm thrilled and lucky to recall. I'm still not 100%, but right enough to deal with some dot com billionaire in Santa Barbara, or more precisely Montecito, and to help recover his fifty mil G5 that's gone missing.

I hope against all hope that he's not an arrogant prick who's impossible to deal with, as I hate to kowtow, even for a seven-figure fee. But I'm sure Hot Springs Road, which is lined with ten million buck and up estates, enjoys the presence of more pricks that the average thirty foot tall Saguaro cactus.

You see, a Grumman, G5, is the ultimate in private business aircraft, and properly appointed, costs a cool fifty million, and this guy, who's so smart in the world of hyperspace was a dummy and didn't have it insured, as there was no lien holder who insisted upon same as Mr. Wedgewood paid cash. He offered a cool million right off the bat, which means to me he'll pay what the recovery is worth, and that's a minimum of five percent, or two and a half million.

After all, those of us who dabble in the recovery biz often command fees up to twenty percent, even higher if the danger coefficient is super high.

I have four vehicles, but don't think it's appropriate to arrive in my van, my F150, or on my Harley Sportster, so I'm driving what I imagine would be considered chic in Montecito, my 1957 tricked out red and white Corvette. After all Lamborghinis, Maseratis, Jags, and Porsches are blasé in and around this posh area of the California coast. Leaving Vegas before dawn, I've enjoyed a leisurely drive over, hearing everything Willy and Whalen have to offer on Sirius and then getting deep into Katy Perry...that's a Freudian slip. It's one of those glorious February days that makes half the world want to migrate to California, temp in the seventies with the hint of a seabreeze, clear, with the offshore islands looking so close you could swim there. It's nice enough that I stopped in Santa Clarita and put the top down on the Vette. As my military cut couldn't be messed up with anything but a razor, I have no worries there, except for the fact I still have a couple of angry scars from splits on my noggin from baseball bats or pipes that a half dozen guys used on me behind a joint called Big Rosie's up in Williston. Both cuts took a dozen stitches to close, and don't add to my boyish good looks. But I yam who I yam, as my fellow Navy type, Popeye, would say...even though I hate to quote a squib.

And I'm as properly attired as I get, in blue blazer with cute brass buttons, powder blue button down shirt, khaki slacks, and brown belt to match my loafers. I'd have gone sockless and worn an ascot—as if I had one—but I'd be afraid one of the local trust fund darlings would pass out from heart palpitations or one of the guys would try to give me a hug upon introduction.

I don't mind a good chest bump, and hoora, if it's a fellow Marine Recon jarhead I served with in Desert Storm, but I draw the line beyond that.

Two Mexican gardeners are working the beds along the one hundred foot drive up to the gate to the Wedgewood estate, and I give them a wave as I pass, and smile when they look surprised. I guess they're used to being invisible to the local gentry.

The fifteen foot tall wrought iron gates blocking my passage, set in an elaborate stone arch flanked by eight foot stone walls, are tipped with gold on top, and the stone guard house probably cost more than the house in which my parents raised me in Sheridan, Wyoming, God rest their souls.

Idling to a stop near an open window facing the driveway, it's all I can do not to smile. I can see a quarter mile beyond the gates through the live oaks and eucalyptus, and still cannot see the house.

The guy behind the guard window doesn't wait, but exits and walks directly to my door. "Mr. Reardon?" he inquires.

And I thought I was nicely dressed, this guy is in a black suit, white shirt and black tie, and the only way you might think he was one of the help as he looks as if he came straight from Gold's Gym before he dressed for work, after he'd done a few reps with about four hundred pounds…and he has on a black bill cap with a big, gold, W embroidered across the front.

"I've got an appointment," I answer.

"May I see a picture ID?" he asks, with steel blue eyes drilling me.

I'm a little surprised to get a glance at something blued hanging under his left arm in a tidy shoulder holster. It's no bigger, I'm happy to note, than the one in the middle of my back. My swinging dick is as big as his.

I produce one of my half dozen driver's licenses, making sure before I hand it over that it's the only legit one of the six and has not only my picture, but Mike

Reardon in the text. He studies it carefully, flashes another long glance at me, then back at the license, back at me, and hands it back.

"You'll have to make this turn around—" for a second I think I'm being dismissed, then he adds—"and go back about a half mile to another gated entrance on the ocean side of the road, that's Birnam Wood Country Club. Mr. Wedgewood is inside and they'll call him out when you arrive, if you'll step into the pro shop and ask. Your meeting is rescheduled for the bar there, or more likely on one of the benches overlooking the course."

I smile, give the well dressed and very polite no-neck guard a nod, and as directed take a turn around the guard house and head back out.

Even though it appears I'm not being allowed to see the house and am being relegated to a bench overlooking the golf course to talk about a seven figure deal, it's too beautiful a day, and much to pretty a drive back down Hot Springs Road with it's overhanging oaks, to get my panties in a twist.

This guardhouse is equally nice, however, the guard here smiles and nods and looks as if he rides his bike to work, and I mean Schwinn not Harley. I give him my name and, without checking my license, he gives me directions to the clubhouse, which I follow. There's a guy under a porte-cochere who's parking cars—if the valet parking sign next to him means anything—in front of a ten thousand or larger square foot club house, although there are no cars awaiting parking. I choose to park myself and do so, and walk to a smaller structure sixty feet to the south of the main building, which, being clever as I am, deduce is the Pro Shop. I guess the putting green at its side was my first clue.

Two guys are working inside, all flashy Colgate smiles as big as those of the little alligators on their shirts, and one of them calls the main building promptly when I introduce myself. Then the younger one escorts me to a bench at the far side of a putting green that looks as if it might have been manicured by a guy with barber's scissors.

As I'm overlooking an equally beautiful golf course, each fairway flanked by multi-million dollar homes, I'm trying to remember what I've read about the place. Had I known our meeting was to take place here, I'd have Googled it, but I have worked out of Santa Barbara quite a bit, and remember reading that Birnam Wood is considered as elite as any East Coast Club, and maybe more so.

There's absolutely no one playing the course, which is not unusual for these very high-end clubs.

I can see up to the main building, and see a tall and surprisingly young man, who looks like Wedgewood's pictures, exit and stride meaningfully down the walk coming the way of the Pro Shop, and as I'm looking back, see another guy, a guy with military bearing, in windbreaker, jeans, and hiking boots, trotting across the parking lot…and although he's tidily dressed, my hackles rise on the back of my neck and I'm instinctively on my feet moving their way.

The young guy looks up in surprise, and surprise turns to fear as the trotter stops in front of him and sticks a corncob-sized finger in his chest. I'm too far still to hear what's being said, but it's being said with a loud voice, and the young guy's eyes are round as saucers. He's wearing a very expensive looking sweater, and just

I near, the big boy gathers it in a wad in hand and backhands the younger one.

Before he can bring the forehand back, I'm on him, grabbing the offending hand with both hands I use a simple Judo takedown, cranking the hand up and inside and putting him on his knees. His surprised look tells he's unused to being under someone's control.

I'm still a long way from being back to full function physically, but I took him from behind and by surprise. I keep the wristlock on him as the young guy who I presume is Wedgeworth sinks to his knees, obviously dazed by the slap.

As I have no idea what's going down, or who the players are, I give the big ol boy on his knees a hard look, press the twist a little tighter, and ask, "Aren't you working way under your weight class here?"

He doesn't answer, but tries to come back against the twist, so I take him to his back, but underestimating him as he manages to spin, hook a toe behind my heel, and kick me a solid one to the knee with the free foot and I go over backward into the azaleas.

We're both clamoring to our feet, but he beats me up as I'm tangled in the greenery, and instead of coming after me, uses the same hiking boot to kick the young guy in the chest, and he does an end'o into the flower beds.

What I presume is some kind of business argument or domestic spat suddenly turns deadly, as I realize he's going to the small of his back under his windbreaker, and we both come up with our automatics at the same instant. We're only ten feet apart and I left my Kevlar home…who'd a thunk it in a place like this?

There's no missing at this range.

About the Author

L. J. Martin is the author of three dozen works of both fiction and non-fiction from Bantam, Avon, Pinnacle and his own Wolfpack Publishing. He lives in Montana with his wife, NYT bestselling romantic suspense author Kat Martin. He's been a horse wrangler, cook as both avocation and vocation, volunteer firefighter, real estate broker, general contractor, appraiser, disaster evaluator for FEMA, and traveled a good part of the world, some in his own ketch. A hunter, fisherman, photographer, cook, father and grandfather, he's been car and plane wrecked, visited a number of *jusgados* and a road camp, and survived cancer twice. He carries a bail-enforcement shield. He knows about what he writes about.

More great action-adventure novels from acclaimed author L. J. Martin

The Repairman.   Got a problem? Mike Reardon, the repairman, can fix it. Your son in debt to his dope dealer? Your captain steal your plane or boat? Someone put a hit on you? Mike Reardon, as a Marine, was taught to search and destroy, now he's got to do what he knows! Acclaimed action adventure writer L. J. Martin brings you the ultimate kick ass fiction...don't pick this one up unless you've got time to read cover to cover.

Windfall.   From the boardroom to the bedroom, David Drake has fought his way...nearly...to the top.   From the jungles of Vietnam, to the vineyards of Napa, to the grit and grime of the California oil fields, he's clawed his way up.   The only thing missing is the woman he's loved most of his life.   Now, he's going to risk it all to win it all, or end up on the very bottom where he started. This business adventure-thriller will leave you breathless.

Quiet Ops.   "...knows crime and how to write about it...you won't put this one down." Elmore Leonard
L. J. Martin with America's No. 1 bounty hunter, Bob Burton, brings action-adventure in double doses.   From Malibu to West Palm Beach, Brad Benedick hooks 'em up and haul 'em in...in chains.

Crimson Hit. Dev Shannon loves his job, travels, makes good money, meets interesting people...then hauls them in cuffs and chains to justice.   Only this time it's personal.

Bullet Blues. Shannon normally doesn't work in his hometown, but this time it's a friend who's gone missing, and he's got to help…if he can stay alive long enough. Tracking down a stolen yacht, which takes him all the way to Jamaica, he finds himself deep in the dirty underbelly of the drug trade.

Venom: A medical thriller. Snake venom can be used to cure…or kill. Dex Reno leaves the Navy Shore Patrol thinking he's taking a cushy job as a campus cop at U.C.L.A…no problem bigger than panty raids and peeping toms…boy, is he in for a surprise. Dope's sold, bullets fly, and snakes slither…not to speak of the distractions of a T & A wonderland. For laughs, shivers, and hot, hot moments, enjoy Venomous.

The Clint Ryan Series:

El Lazo. John Clinton Ryan, young, fresh to the sea from Mystic, Connecticut, is shipwrecked on the California coast…and blamed for the catastrophe. Hunted by the hide, horn and tallow captains, he escapes into the world of the vaquero, and soon gains the name El Lazo, for his skill with the lasso. A classic western tale of action and adventure, and the start of the John Clinton Ryan, the Clint Ryan series.

Against the 7th Flag. Clint Ryan, now skilled with horse and reata, finds himself caught up in the war of California revolution, Manifest Destiny is on the march, and he's in the middle of the fray, with friends on one side and countrymen on the other…it's fight or be killed, but for whom?

The Devil's Bounty. On a trip to buy horses for his new ranch in the wilds of swampy Central California, Clint finds himself compelled to help a rich Californio don who's beautiful daughter has been kidnapped and hauled to the barracoons of the Barbary Coast. Thrown in among the Chinese tongs, Australian Sidney Ducks, and the dredges of the gold rush failures, he soon finds an ally in a slave, now a newly freedman, and it's gunsmoke and flashing blades to fight his way to free the senorita.

The Benicia Belle. Clint signs on as master-at-arms on a paddle wheeler plying the Sacramento from San Francisco to the gold fields. He's soon blackmailed by the boats owner and drawn to a woman as dangerous and beautiful as the sea he left behind. Framed for a crime he didn't commit, he has only one chance to exact a measure of justice and…revenge.

Shadow of the Grizzly. "Martin has produced a landlocked, Old West version of Peter Benchley's *Jaws*," Publisher's Weekly. When the Stokes brothers, the worst kind of meat hunters, stumble on Clint's horse ranch, they are looking to take what he has. A wounded griz is only trying to stay alive, but he's a horrible danger to man and beast. And it's Clint, and his crew, including a young boy, who face hell together.

Condor Canyon. On his way to Los Angeles, a pueblo of only one thousand, Clint is ambushed by a posse after the abductor of a young woman. Soon he finds himself trading his Colt and his skill for the horses he seeks…now if he can only stay alive to claim them.

The Montana Series – The Clan:

Stranahan. "A good solid fish-slinging gunslinging read," William W. Johnstone. Sam Stranahan's an honest man who finds himself on the wrong side of the law, and the law has their own version of right and wrong. He's on his way to find his brother, and walks into an explosive case of murder. He has to make sure justice is done…with or without the law.

McCreed's Law. Gone…a shipment of gold and a handful of passengers from the Transcontinental Railroad. Found…a man who knows the owlhoots and the Indians who are holding the passengers for ransom. When you want to catch outlaws, hire an outlaw…and get the hell out of the way.

Wolf Mountain. The McQuades are running cattle, while running from the tribes who are fresh from killing Custer, and they know no fear. They have a rare opportunity, to get a herd to Mile's and his troops at the mouth of the Tongue…or to die trying. And a beautiful woman and her father, of questionable background, who wander into camp look like a blessing, but trouble is close on their trail…as if the McQuades don't have trouble enough.

O'Rourke's Revenge. Surviving the notorious Yuma Prison should be enough trouble for any man…but Ryan

O'Rourke is not just any man. He wants blood, the blood of those who framed him for a crime he didn't commit. He plans to extract revenge, if it costs him all he has left, which is less than nothing...except his very life.

McKeag's Mountain. Old Bertoldus Prager has long wanted McKeag's Mountain, the Lucky Seven Ranch his father had built, and seven hired guns tried to take it the hard way, leaving Dan McKeag for dead...but he's a McKeag, and clings to life. They should have made sure...for now it will cost them all, or he'll die trying, and Prager's in his sights as well.

The Nemesis Series:

Nemesis. The fools killed his family...then made him a lawman! There are times when it pays not to be known, for if they had, they'd have killed him on the spot. He hadn't seen his sister since before the war, and never met her husband and two young daughters...but when he heard they'd been murdered, it was time to come down out of the high country and scatter the country with blood and guts.

Mr. Pettigrew. Beau Boone, starving, half a left leg, at the end of his rope, falls off the train in the hell-on-wheels town of Nemesis. But Mr. Pettigrew intervenes. Beau owes him, but does he owe him his very life? Can a one-legged man sit shotgun in one of the toughest saloons on the Transcontinental. He can, if he doesn't have anything to lose.

The Ned Cody Series:

Buckshot.   Young Ned Cody takes the job as City Marshal…after all, he's from a long line of lawmen. But they didn't face a corrupt sheriff and his half-dozen hard deputies, a half-Mexican half-Indian killer, and a town who thinks he could never do the job.

Mojave Showdown.   Ned Cody goes far out of his jurisdiction when one of his deputies is hauled into the hell's fire of the Mojave Desert by a tattooed Indian who could track a deer fly and live on his leavings. He's the toughest of the tough, and the Mojave has produced the worst. It's ride into the jaws of hell, and don't worry about coming back.

About the Author

L. J. Martin is the author of three dozen works of both fiction and non-fiction from Bantam, Avon, Pinnacle and his own Wolfpack Publishing. He lives in Montana wtih his wife, NYT bestselling romantic suspense author Kat Martin. He's been a horse wrangler, cook as both avocation and vocation, volunteer firefighter, real estate broker, general contractor, appraiser, disaster evaluator for FEMA, and traveled a good part of the world, some in his own ketch. A hunter, fisherman, photographer, cook, father and grandfather, he's been car and plane wrecked, visited a number of *jusgados* and a road camp, and survived cancer twice. He carries a bail-enforcement shield. He knows about what he writes about.

Join him on facebook at L. J. Martin, on Twitter at #westwrite, and on youtube as ljmartinwolfpack.

Search Amazon and other bookseller sites for his many novels in both print and eBook.

Made in the USA
Charleston, SC
19 May 2014